The Great Pancake Escape

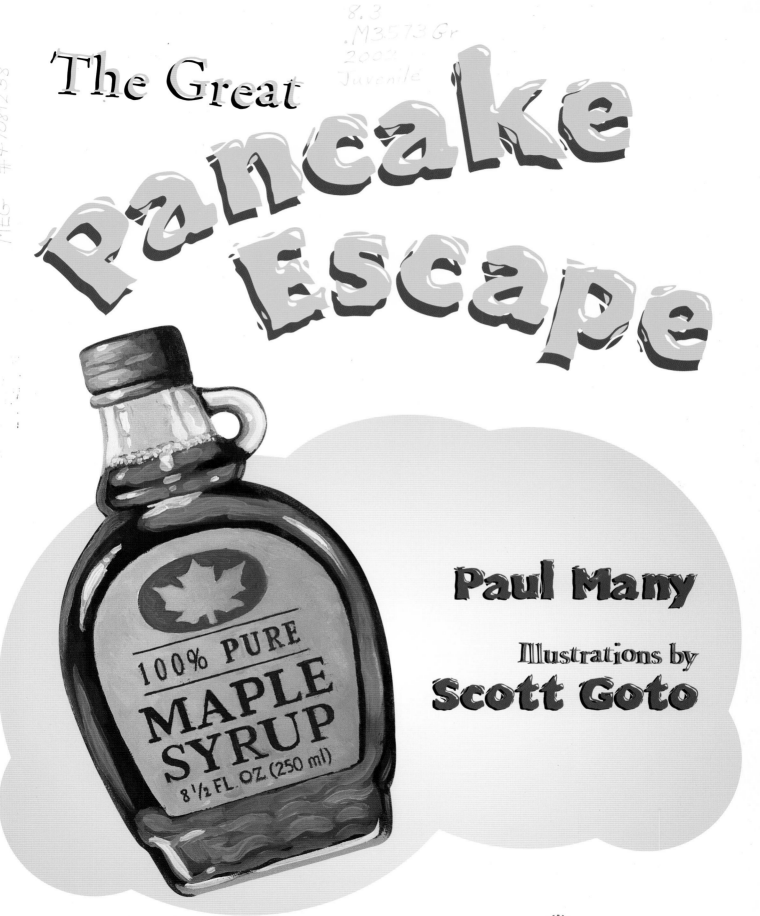

100% PURE MAPLE SYRUP
8 ½ FL. OZ. (250 ml)

Paul Many

Illustrations by
Scott Goto

Walker & Company New York

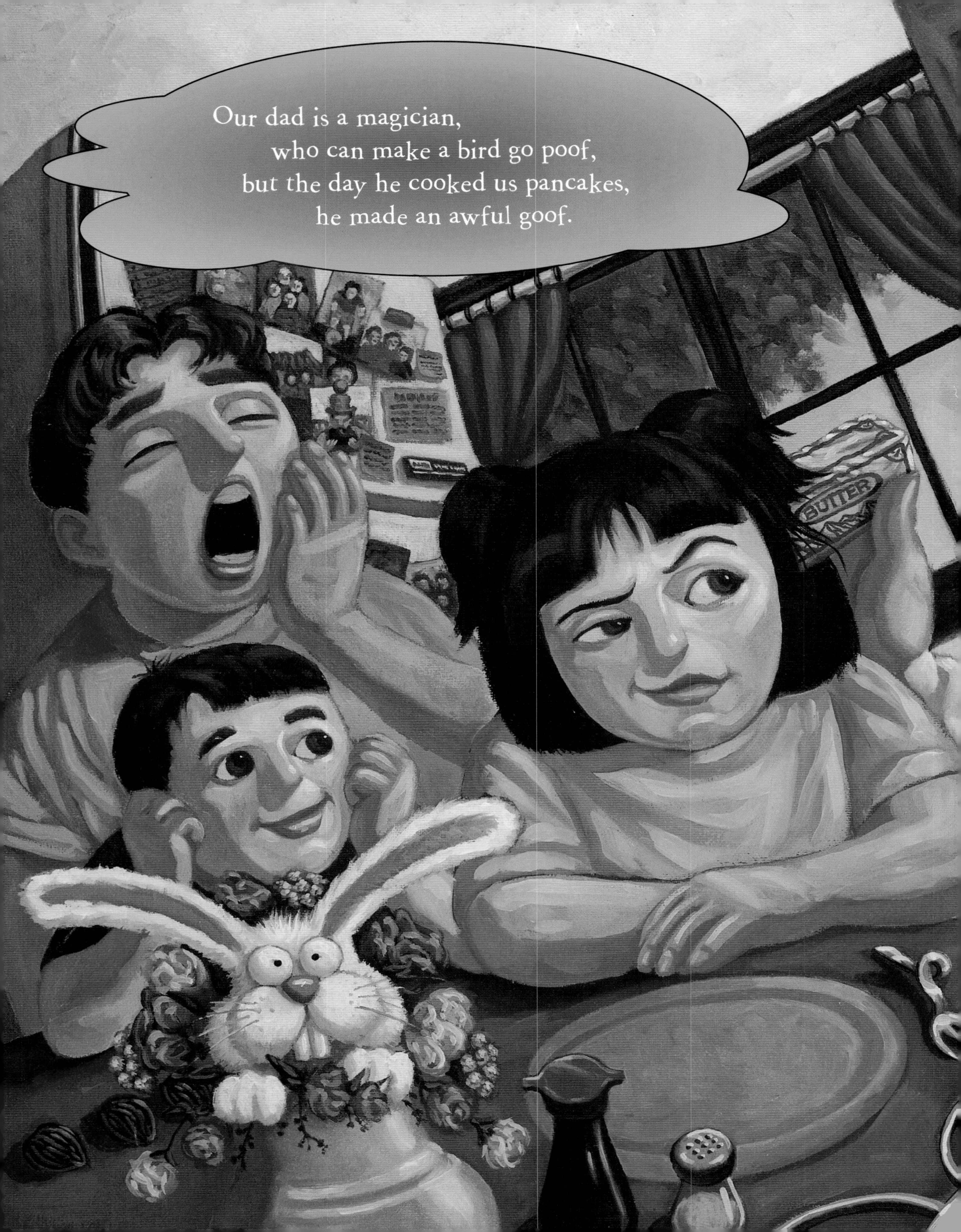
Our dad is a magician,
who can make a bird go poof,
but the day he cooked us pancakes,
he made an awful goof.
BUTTER

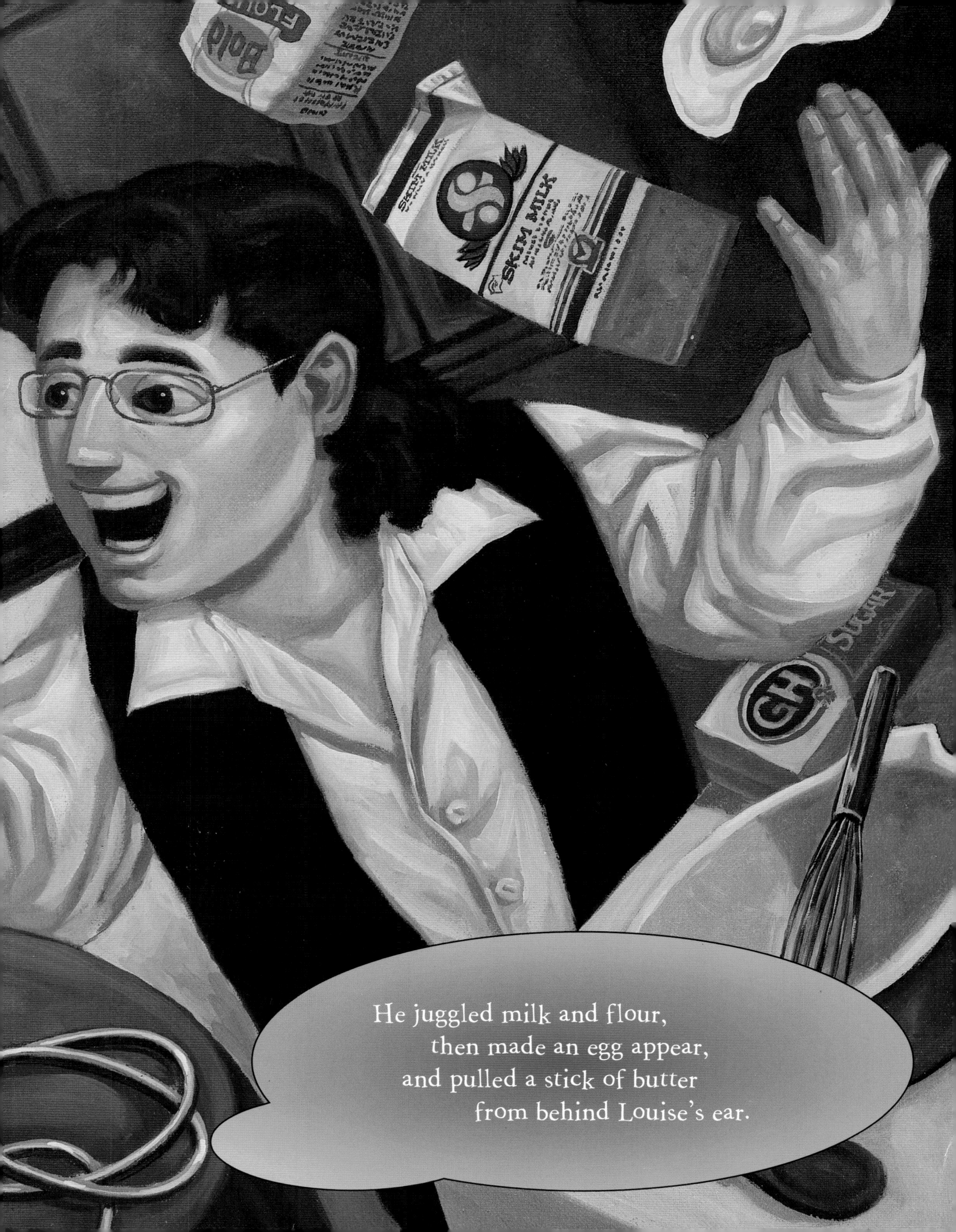
FLOUR
SKIM MILK
SKIM MILK
SUGAR
GH

He juggled milk and flour,
then made an egg appear,
and pulled a stick of butter
from behind Louise's ear.

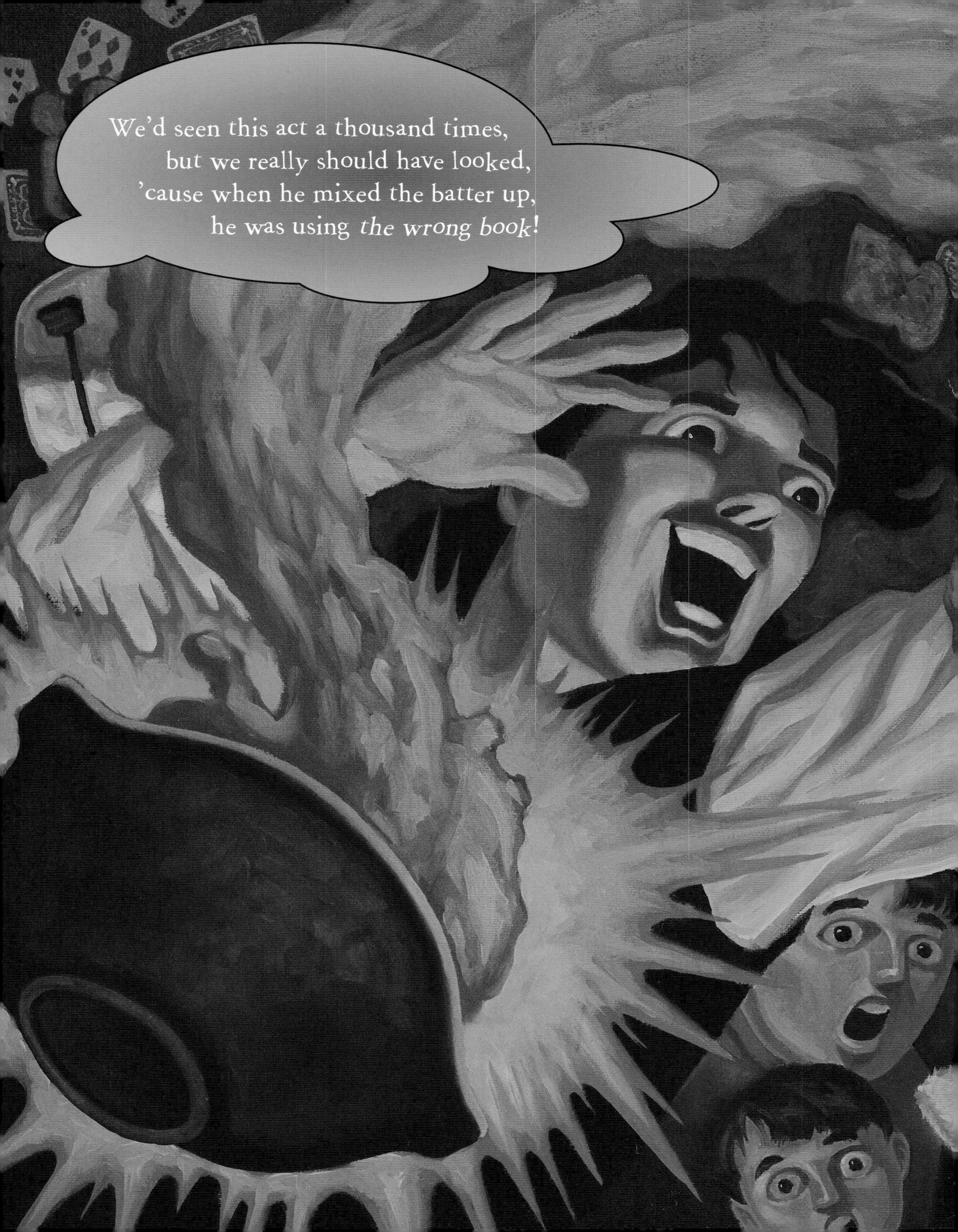
We'd seen this act a thousand times,
but we really should have looked,
'cause when he mixed the batter up,
he was using *the wrong book*!

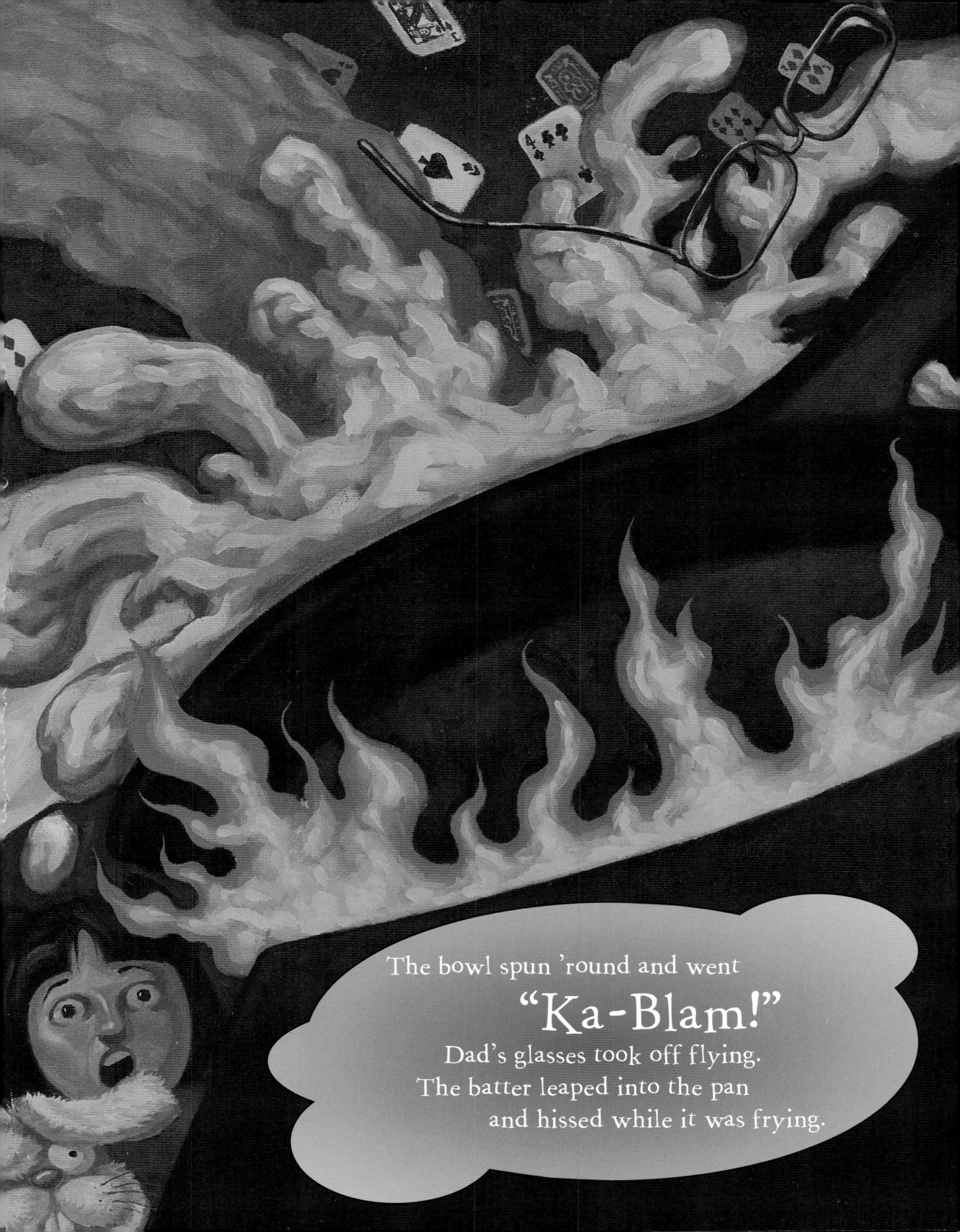

The bowl spun 'round and went
"Ka-Blam!"
Dad's glasses took off flying.
The batter leaped into the pan
and hissed while it was frying.

The stove belched smoke and fire;
the pancakes leaped and hopped.
We dove beneath the tabletop
and shouted, "Watch out, Pop!"

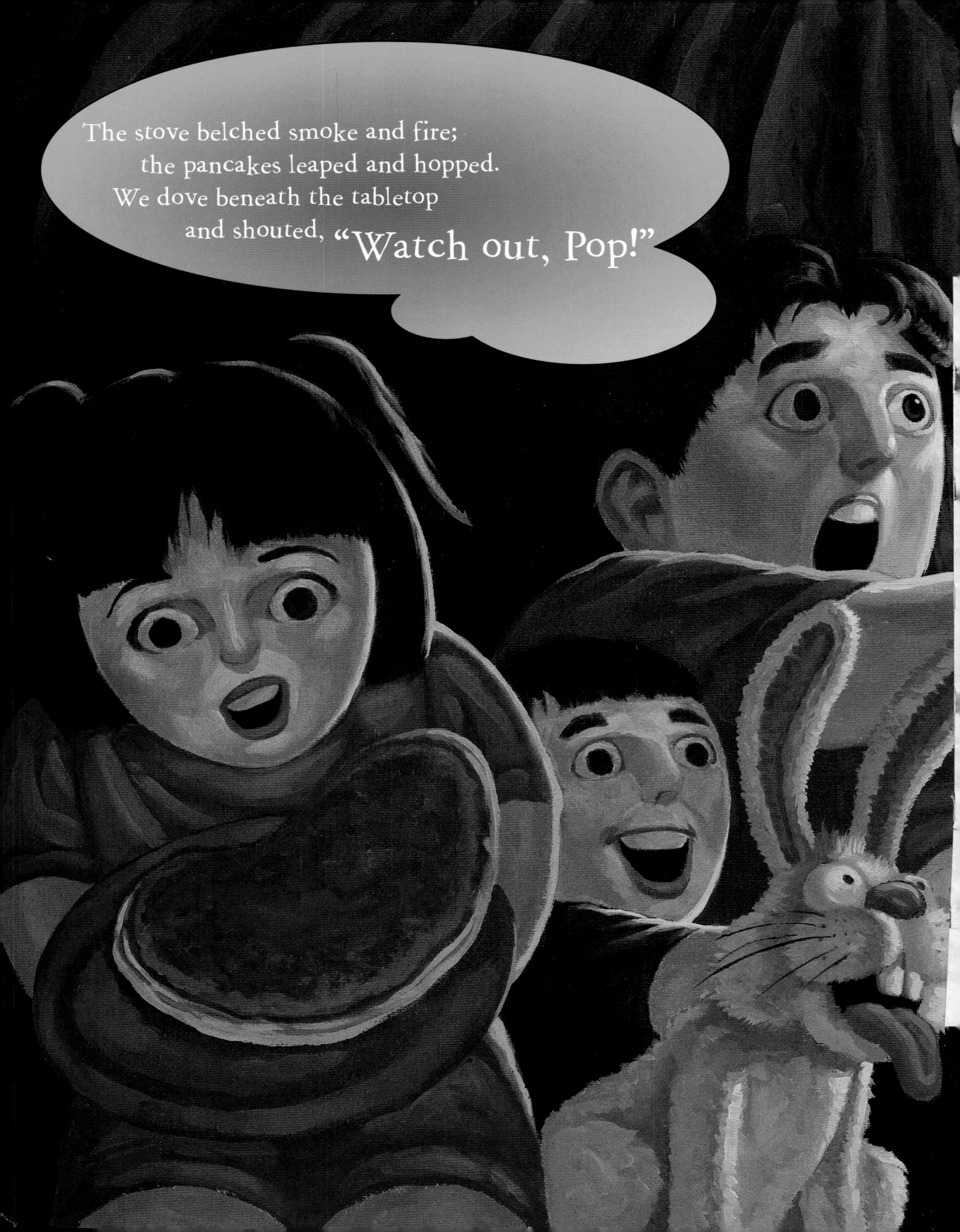

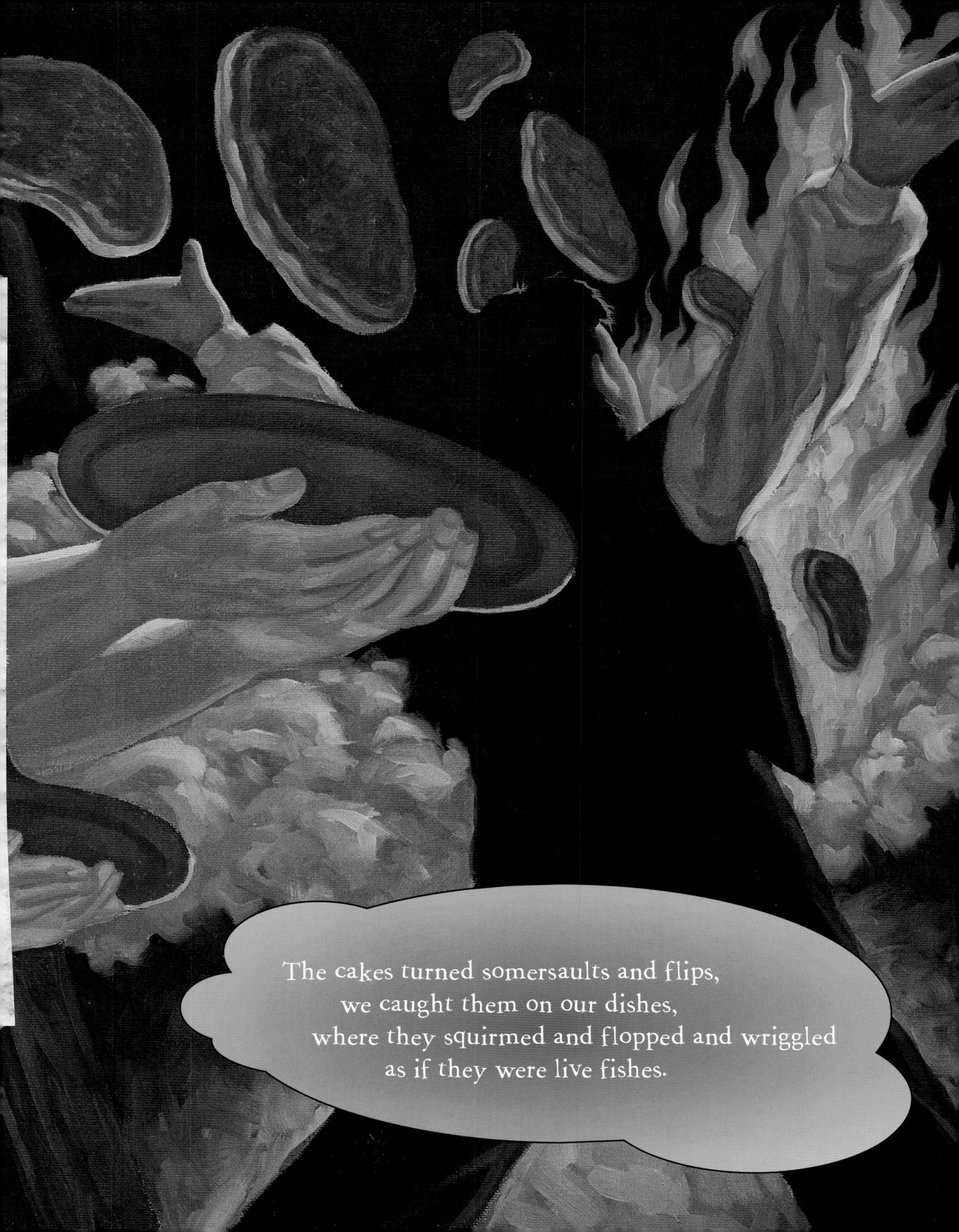
The cakes turned somersaults and flips,
we caught them on our dishes,
where they squirmed and flopped and wriggled
as if they were live fishes.

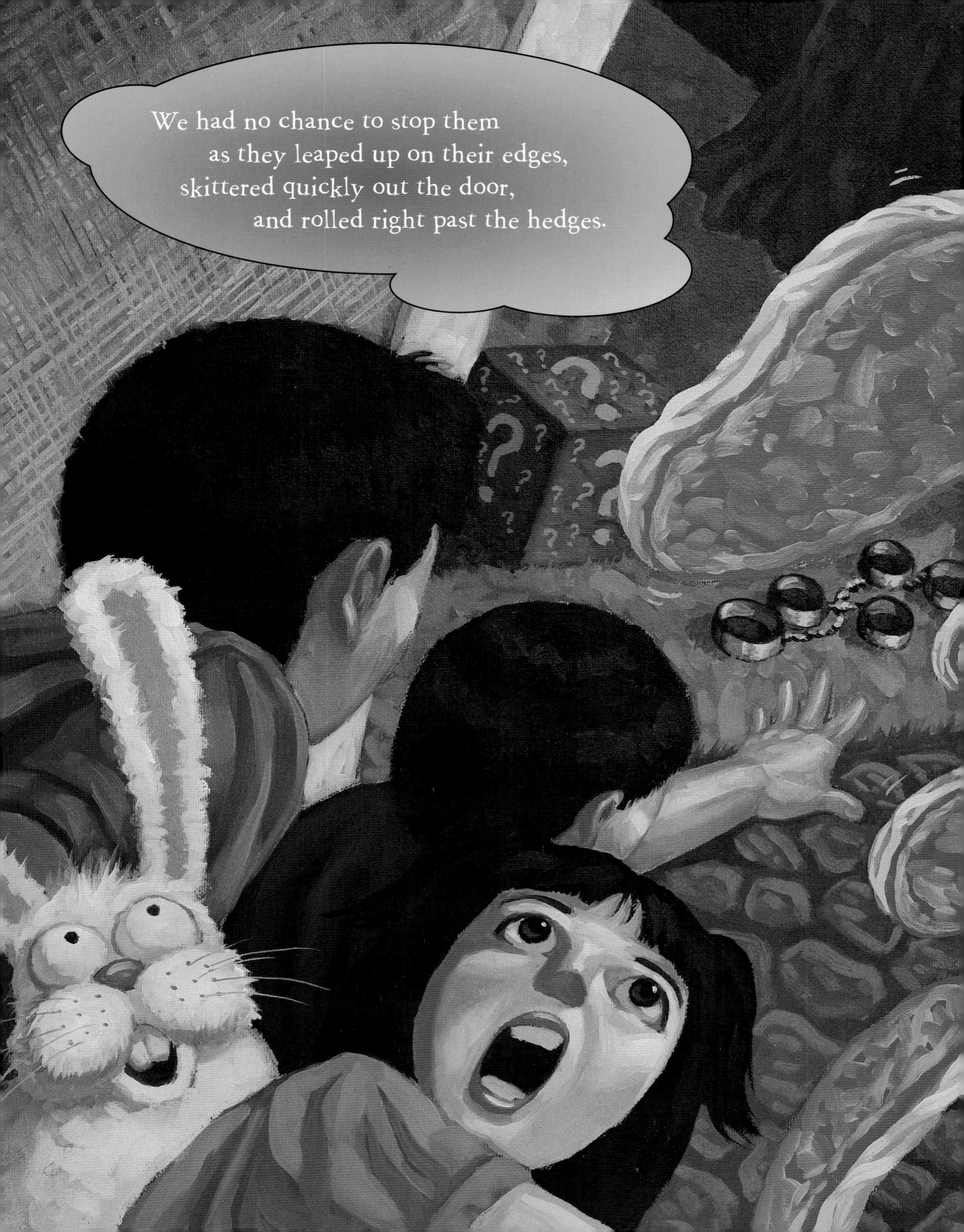
We had no chance to stop them
as they leaped up on their edges,
skittered quickly out the door,
and rolled right past the hedges.

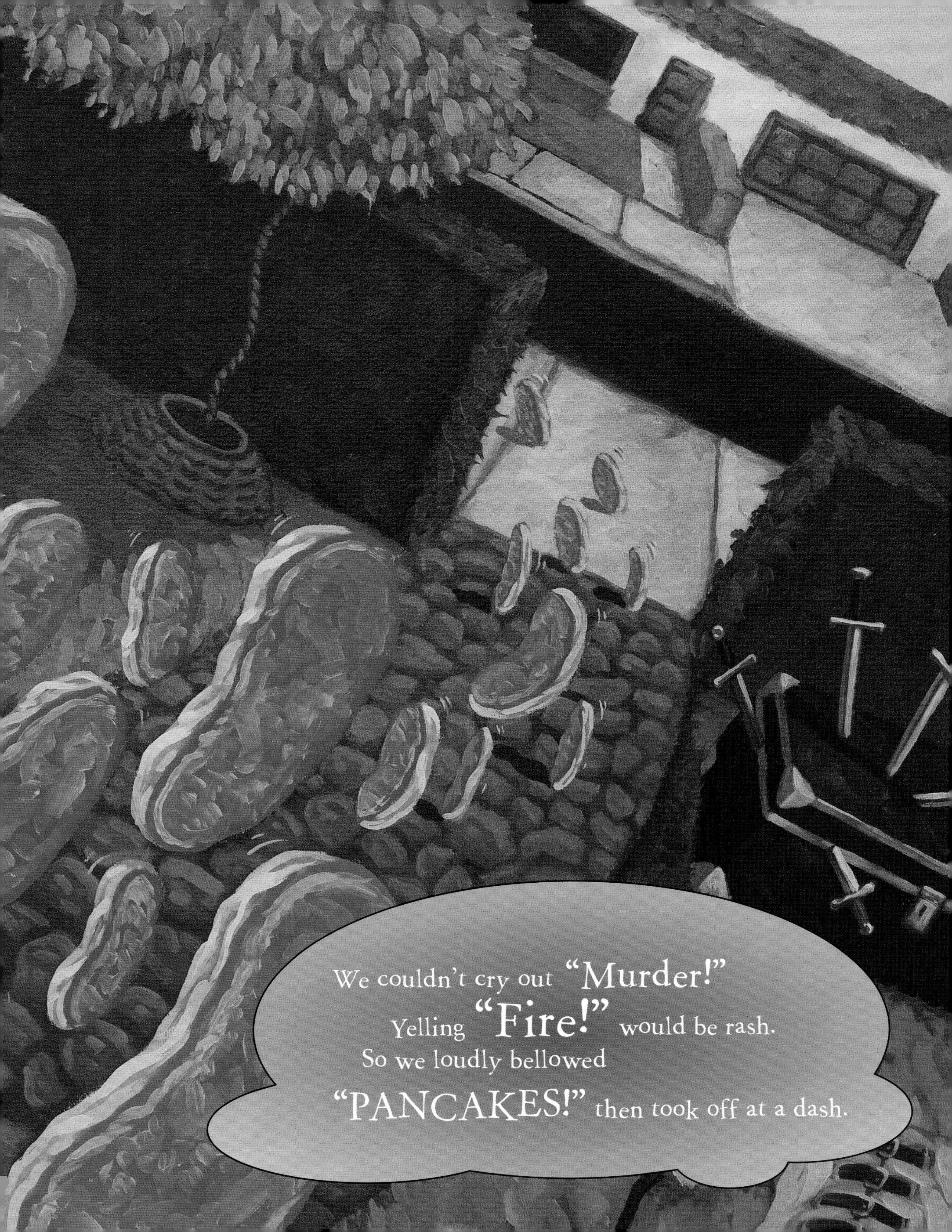

We couldn't cry out "Murder!"
Yelling "Fire!" would be rash.
So we loudly bellowed
"PANCAKES!" then took off at a dash.

They shot on down the driveway,
where they spun around the cats.
Flying through the mailman's legs,
they flipped like acrobats.

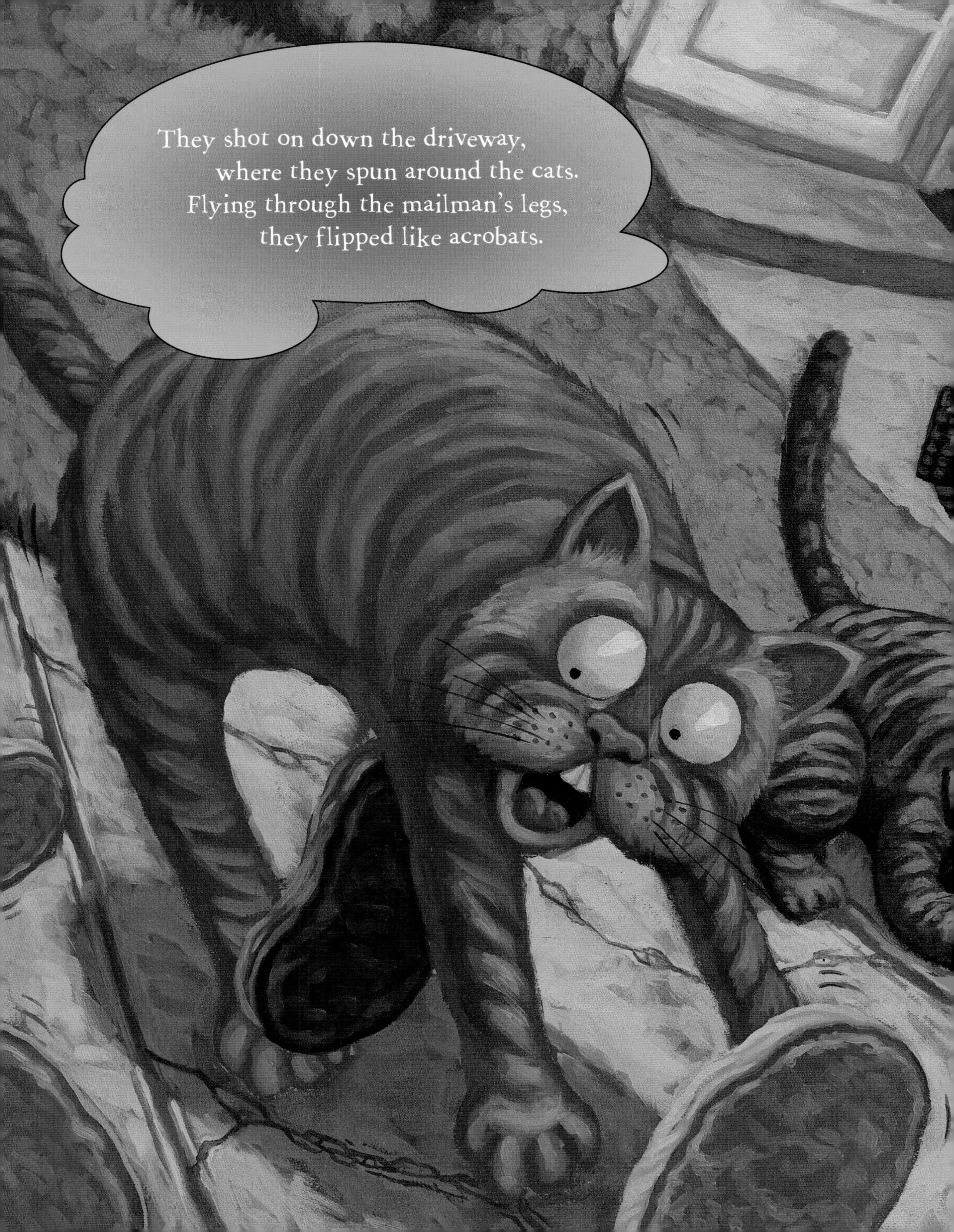

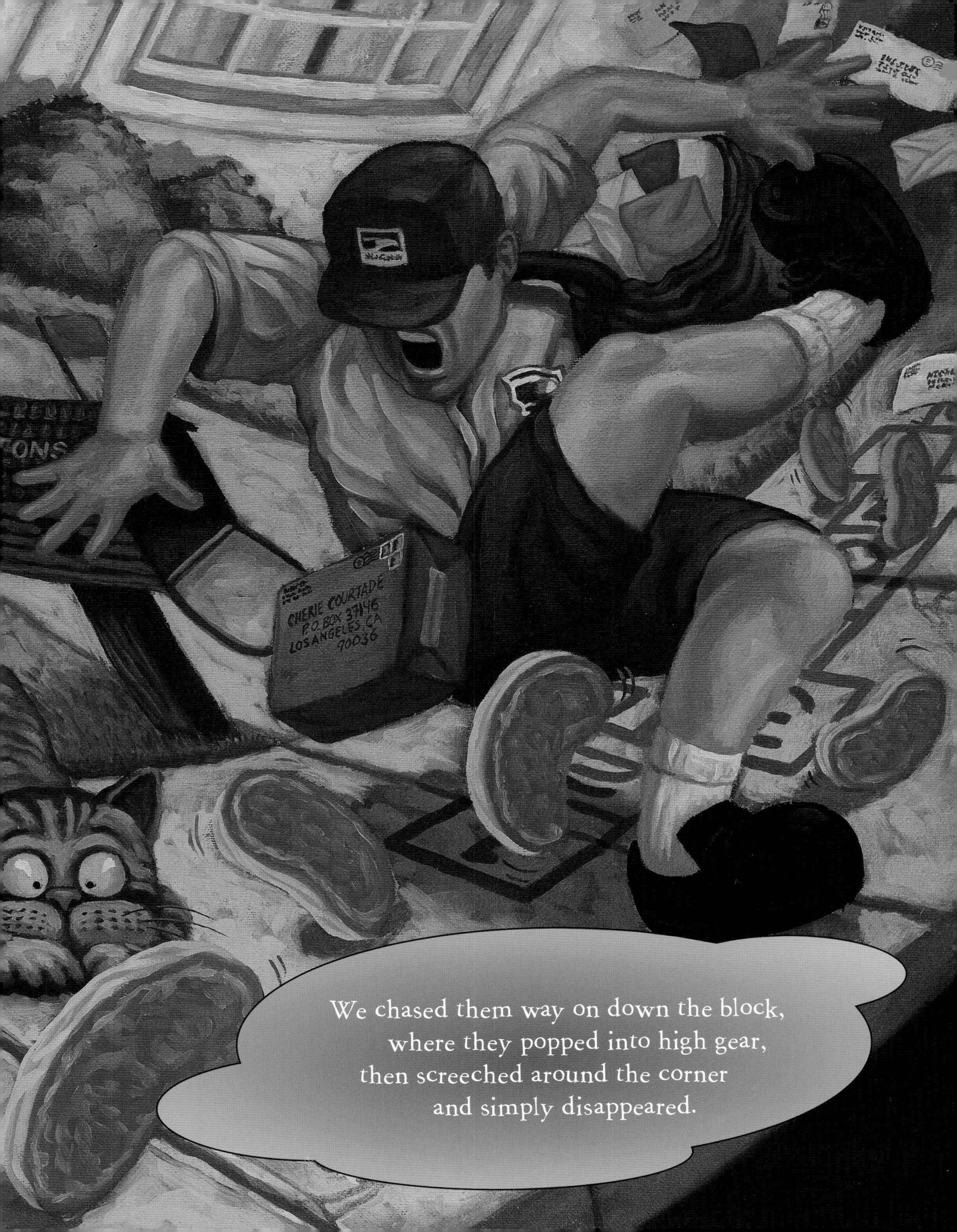
CHERIE COURTADE
P.O. BOX 37146
LOS ANGELES, CA
90036

We chased them way on down the block,
where they popped into high gear,
then screeched around the corner
and simply disappeared.

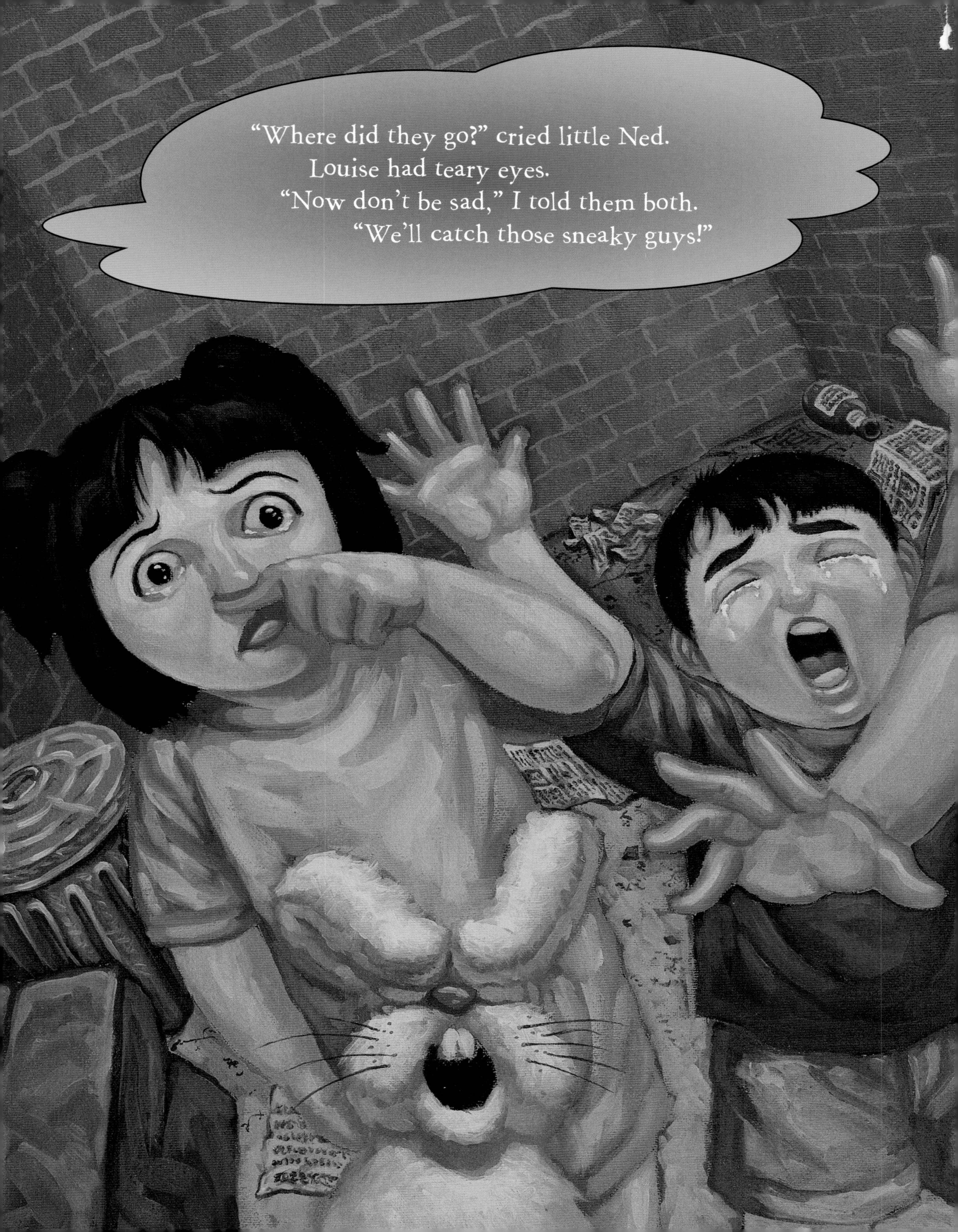
"Where did they go?" cried little Ned.
Louise had teary eyes.
"Now don't be sad," I told them both.
"We'll catch those sneaky guys!"

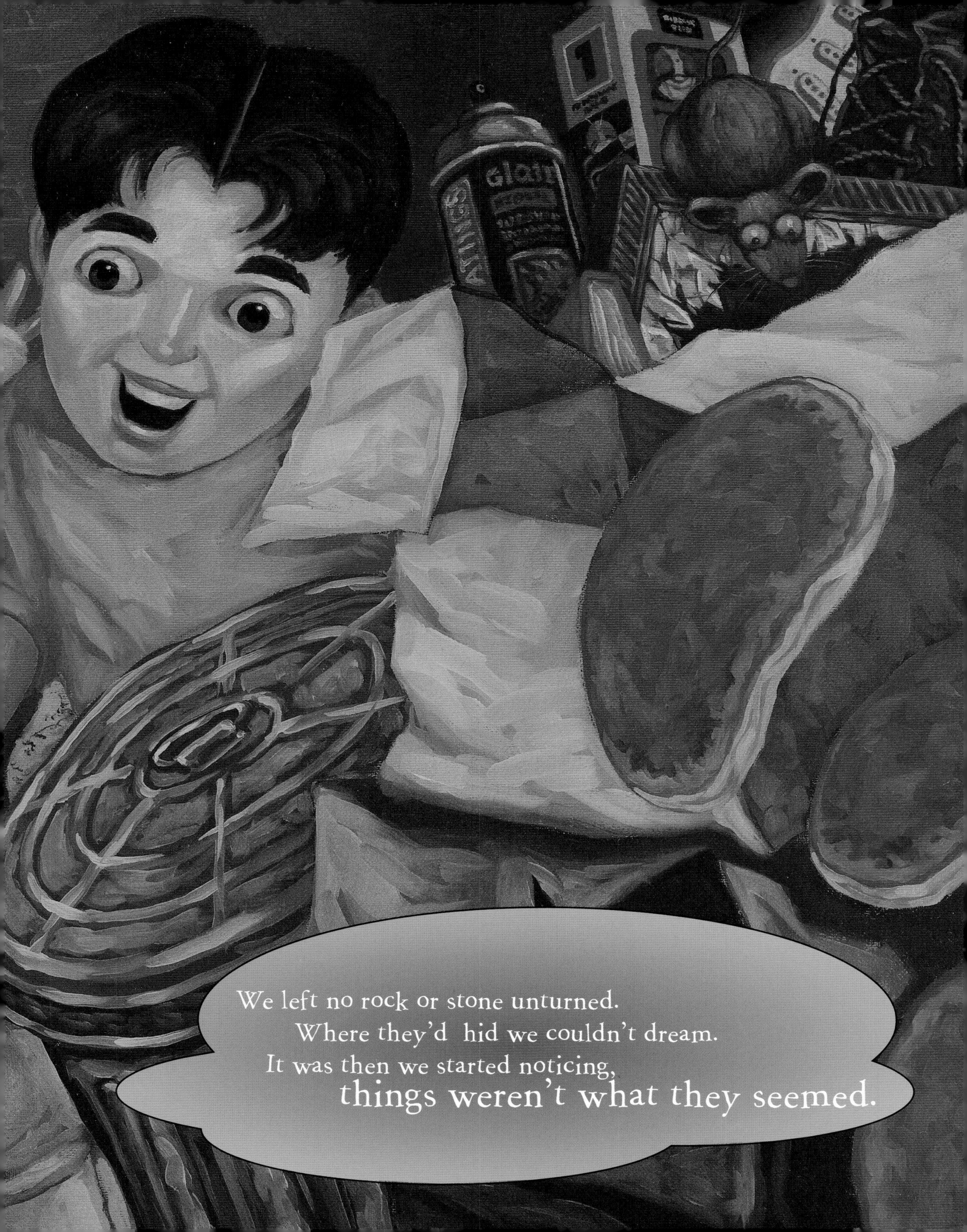
We left no rock or stone unturned.
Where they'd hid we couldn't dream.
It was then we started noticing,
things weren't what they seemed.

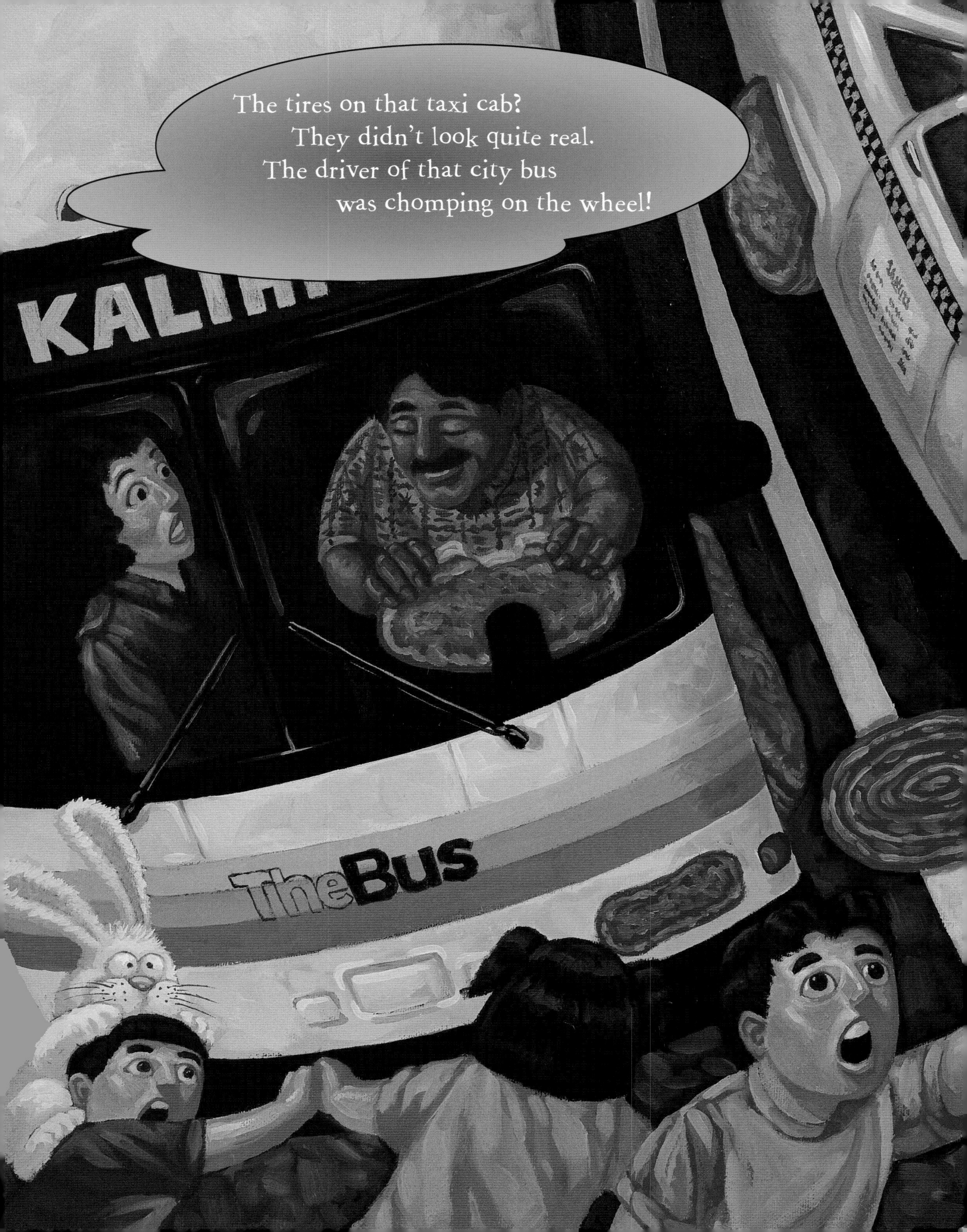
The tires on that taxi cab?
They didn't look quite real.
The driver of that city bus
was chomping on the wheel!
TheBus

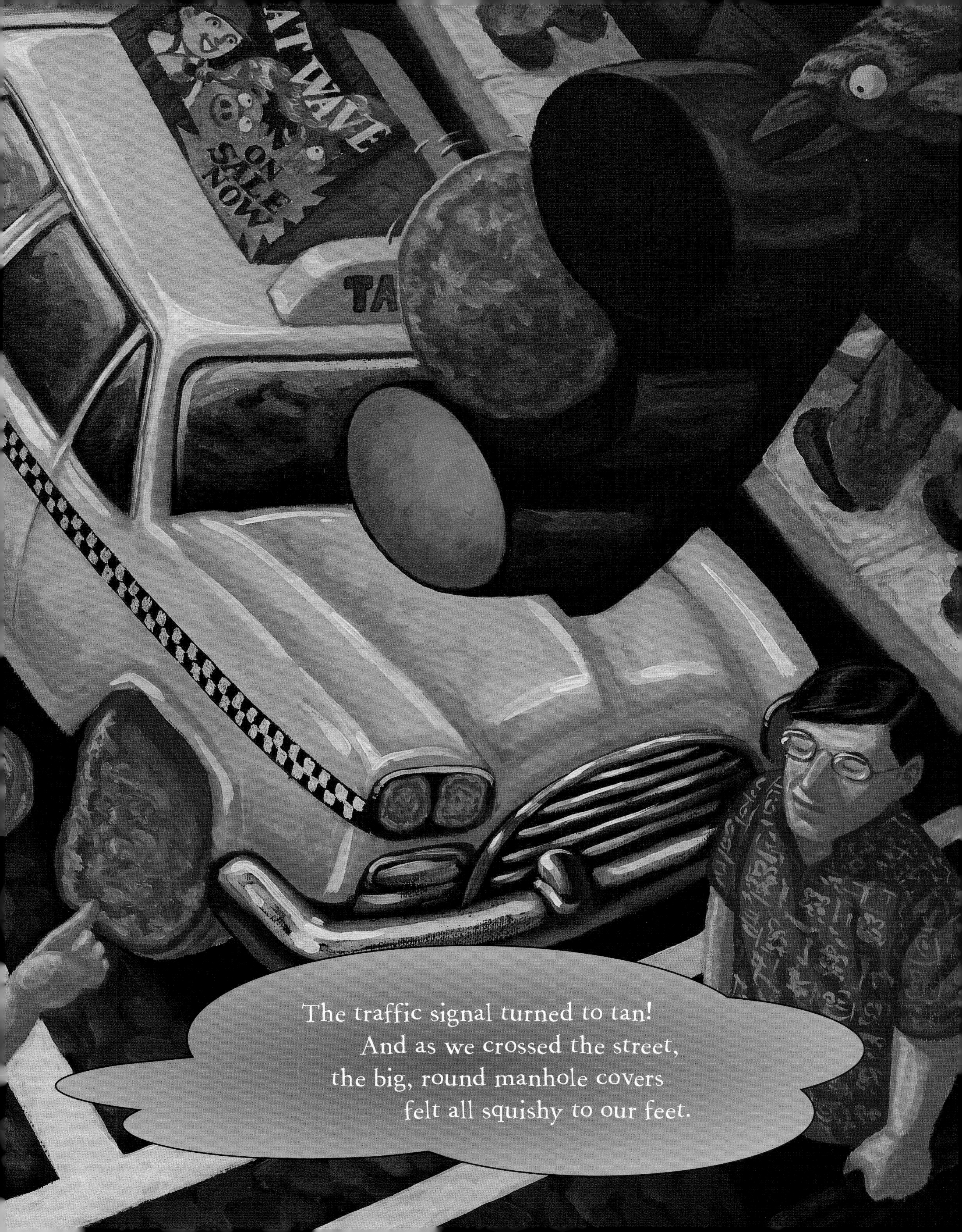
ATWAVE
ON SALE NOW
TA

The traffic signal turned to tan!
And as we crossed the street,
the big, round manhole covers
felt all squishy to our feet.

A highfalutin lady
strolled into our view
in a funny hat that looked
good enough to chew.

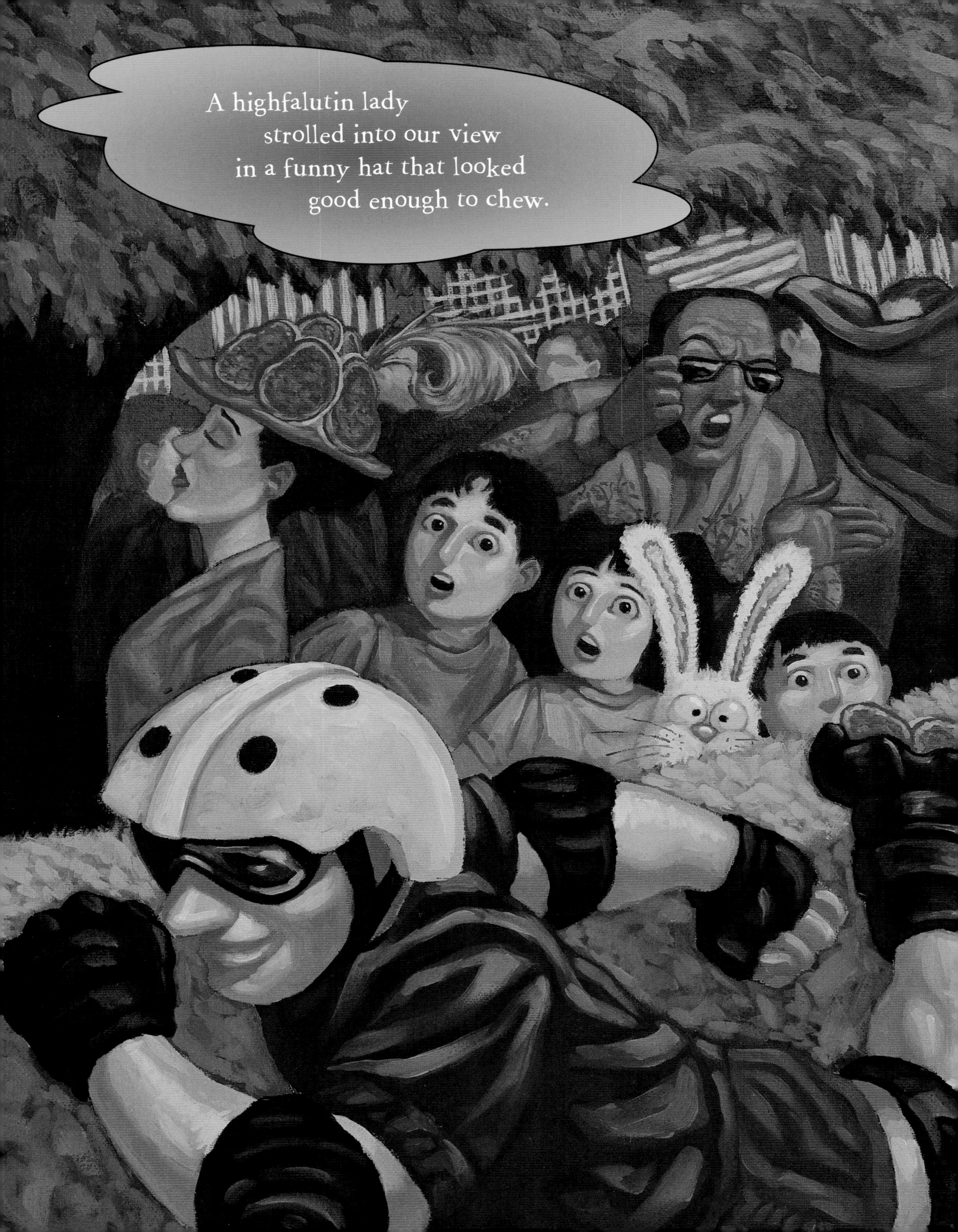

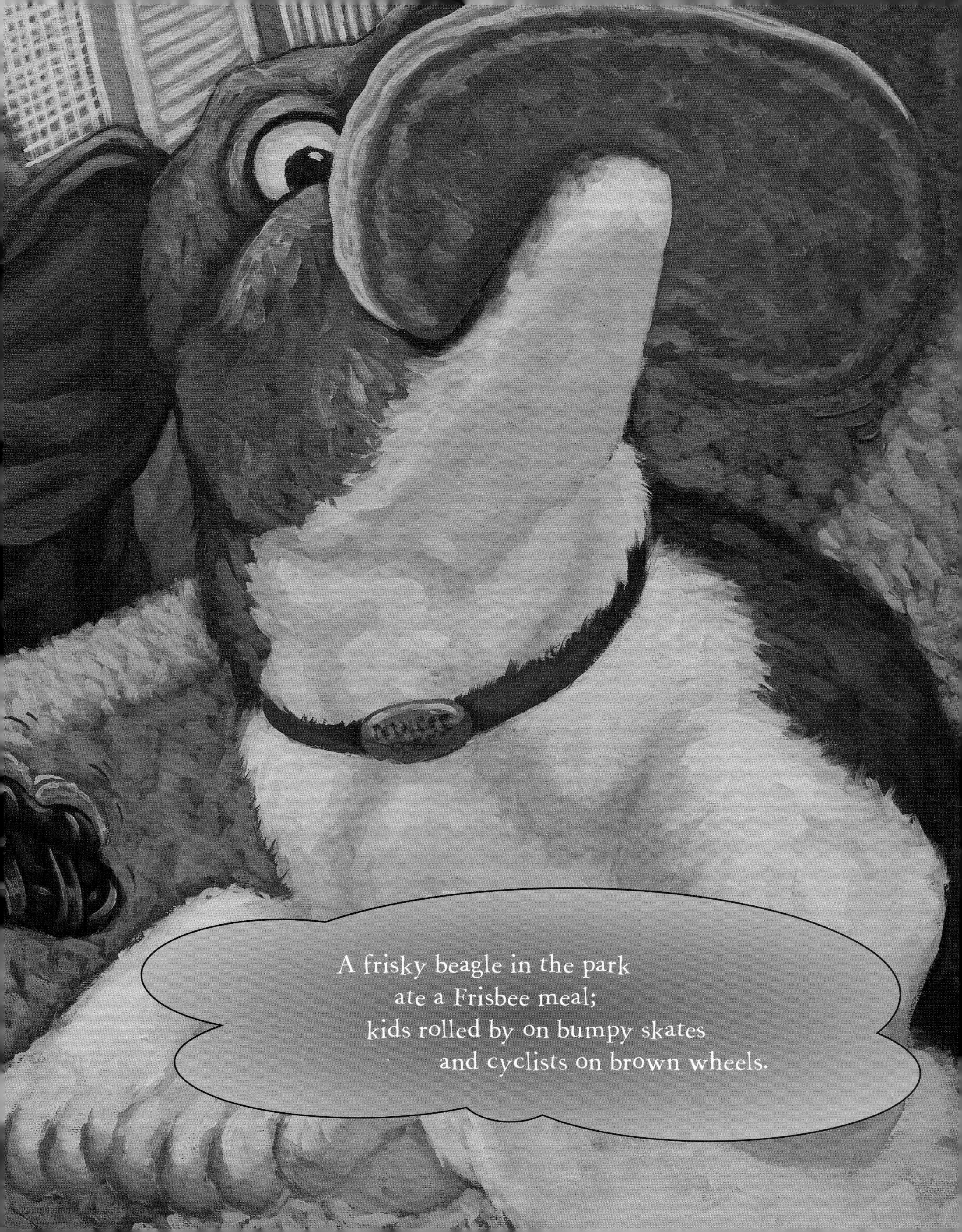

A frisky beagle in the park
ate a Frisbee meal;
kids rolled by on bumpy skates
and cyclists on brown wheels.

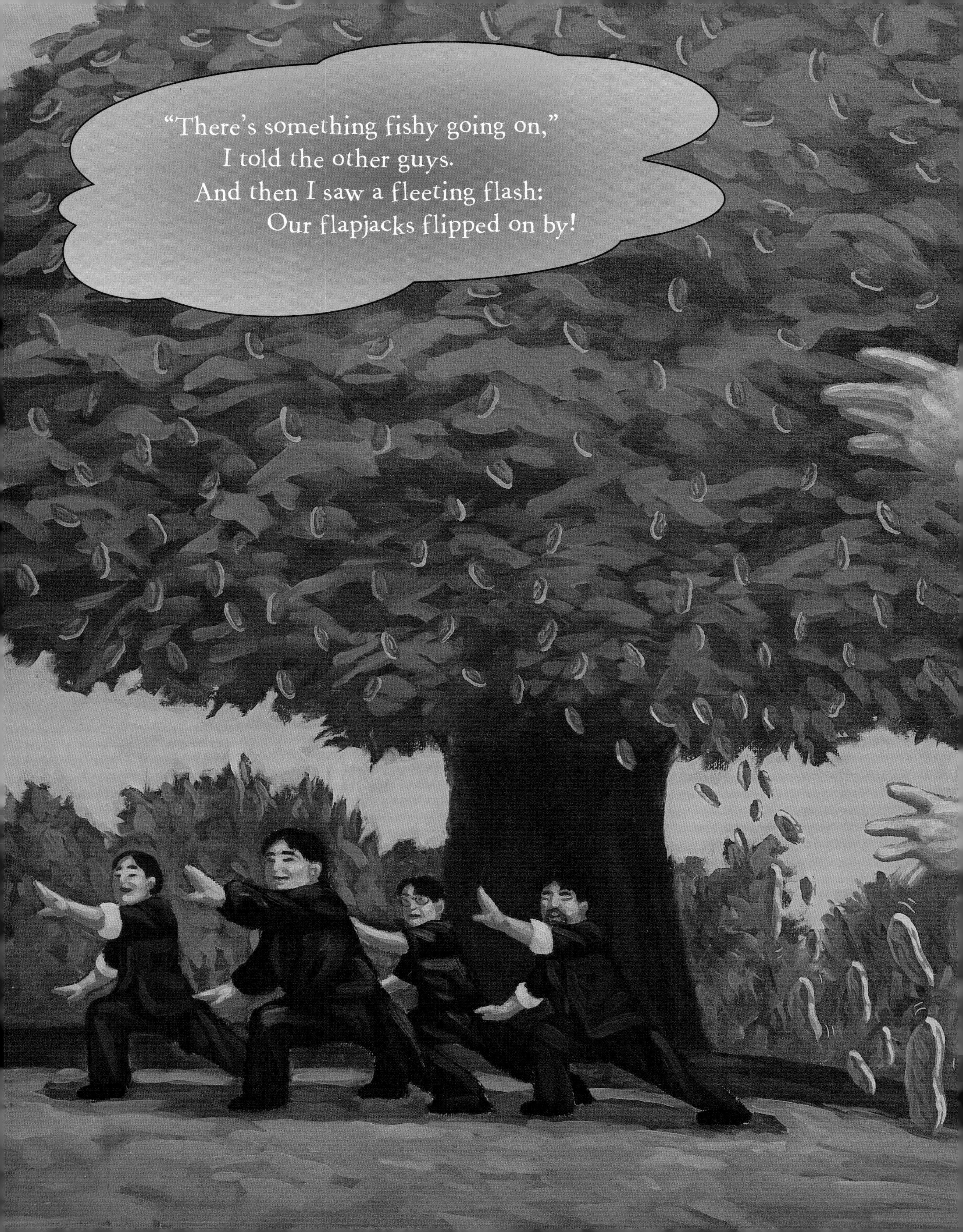
"There's something fishy going on,"
I told the other guys.
And then I saw a fleeting flash:
Our flapjacks flipped on by!

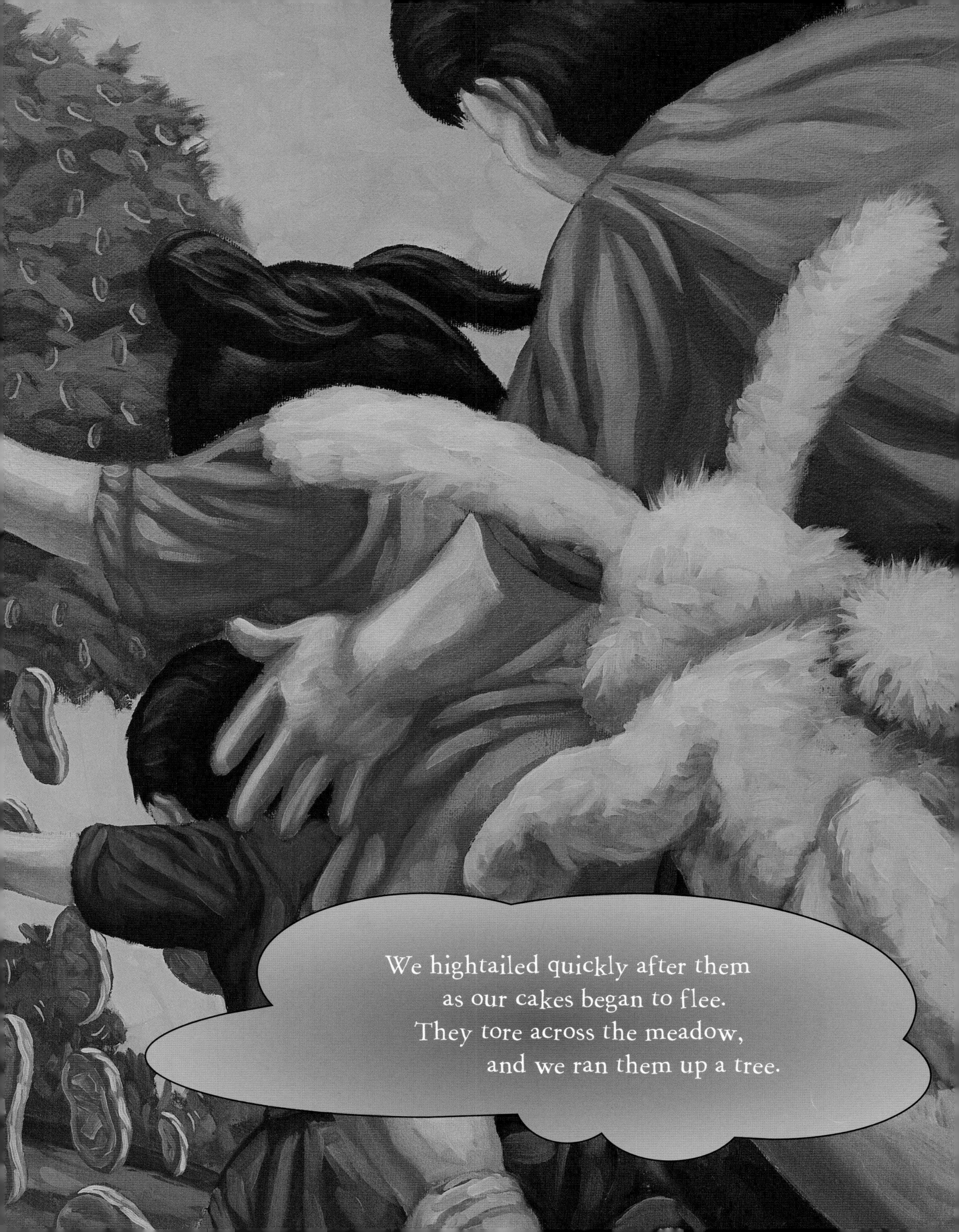
We hightailed quickly after them
as our cakes began to flee.
They tore across the meadow,
and we ran them up a tree.

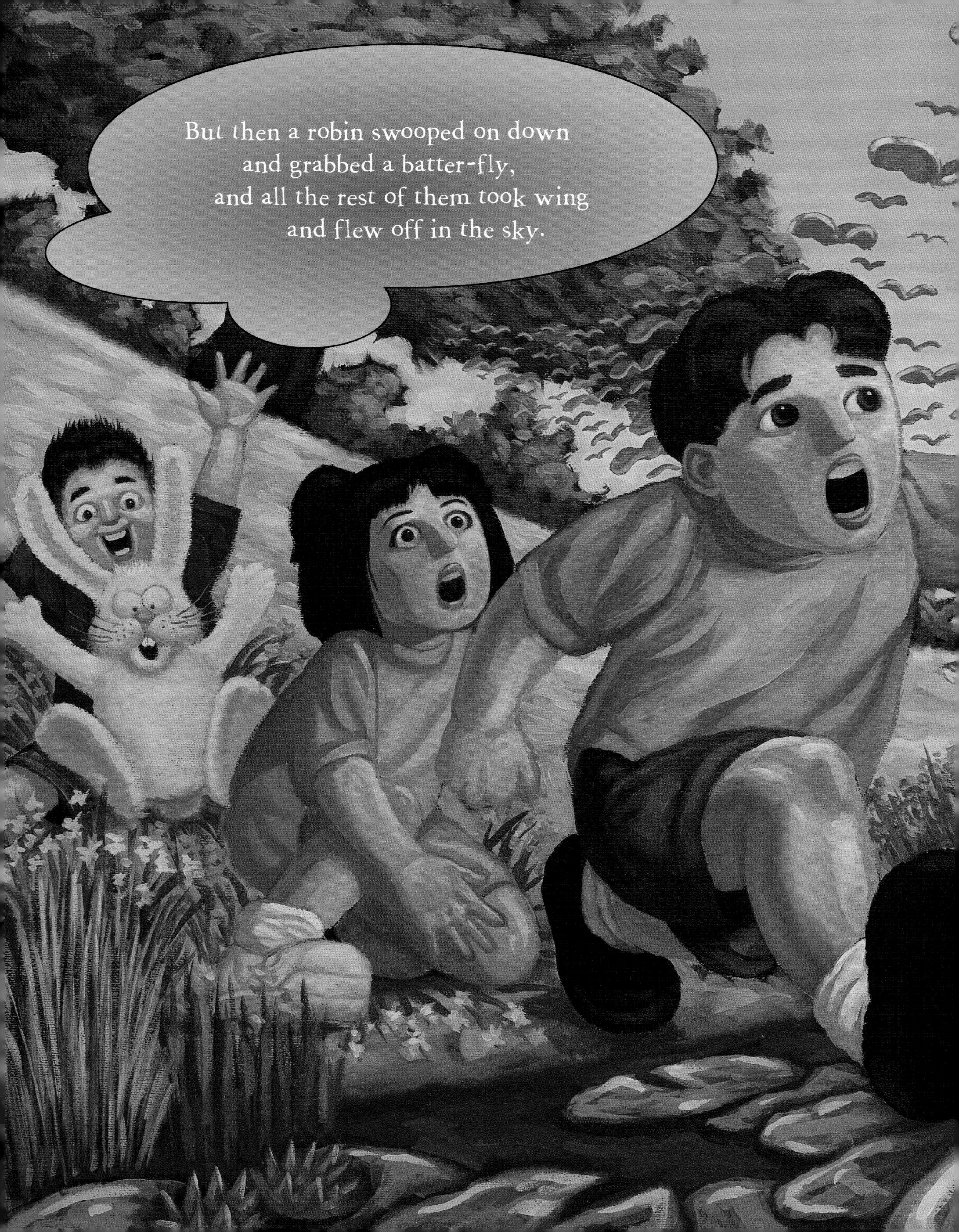
But then a robin swooped on down
and grabbed a batter-fly,
and all the rest of them took wing
and flew off in the sky.

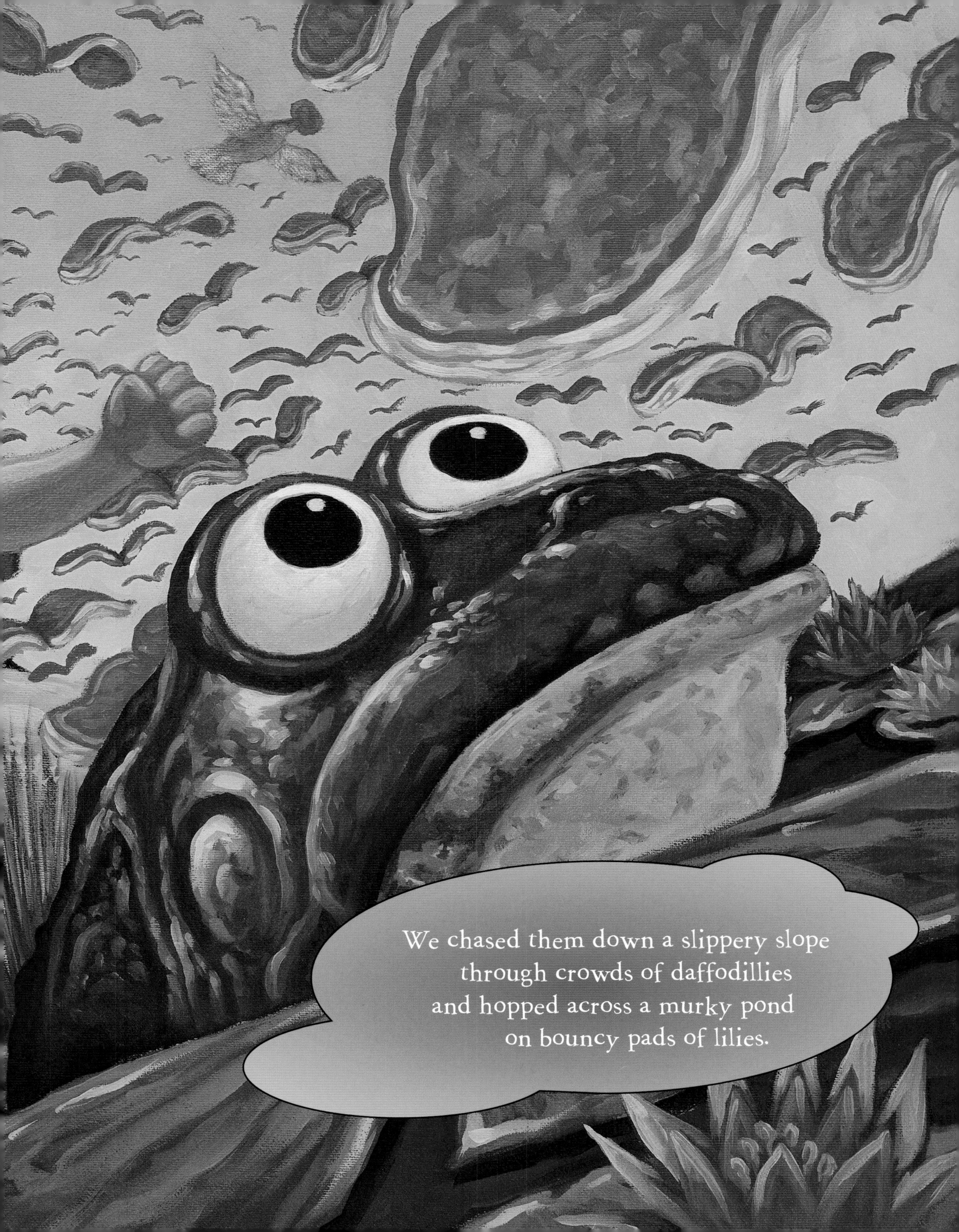
We chased them down a slippery slope
through crowds of daffodillies
and hopped across a murky pond
on bouncy pads of lilies.

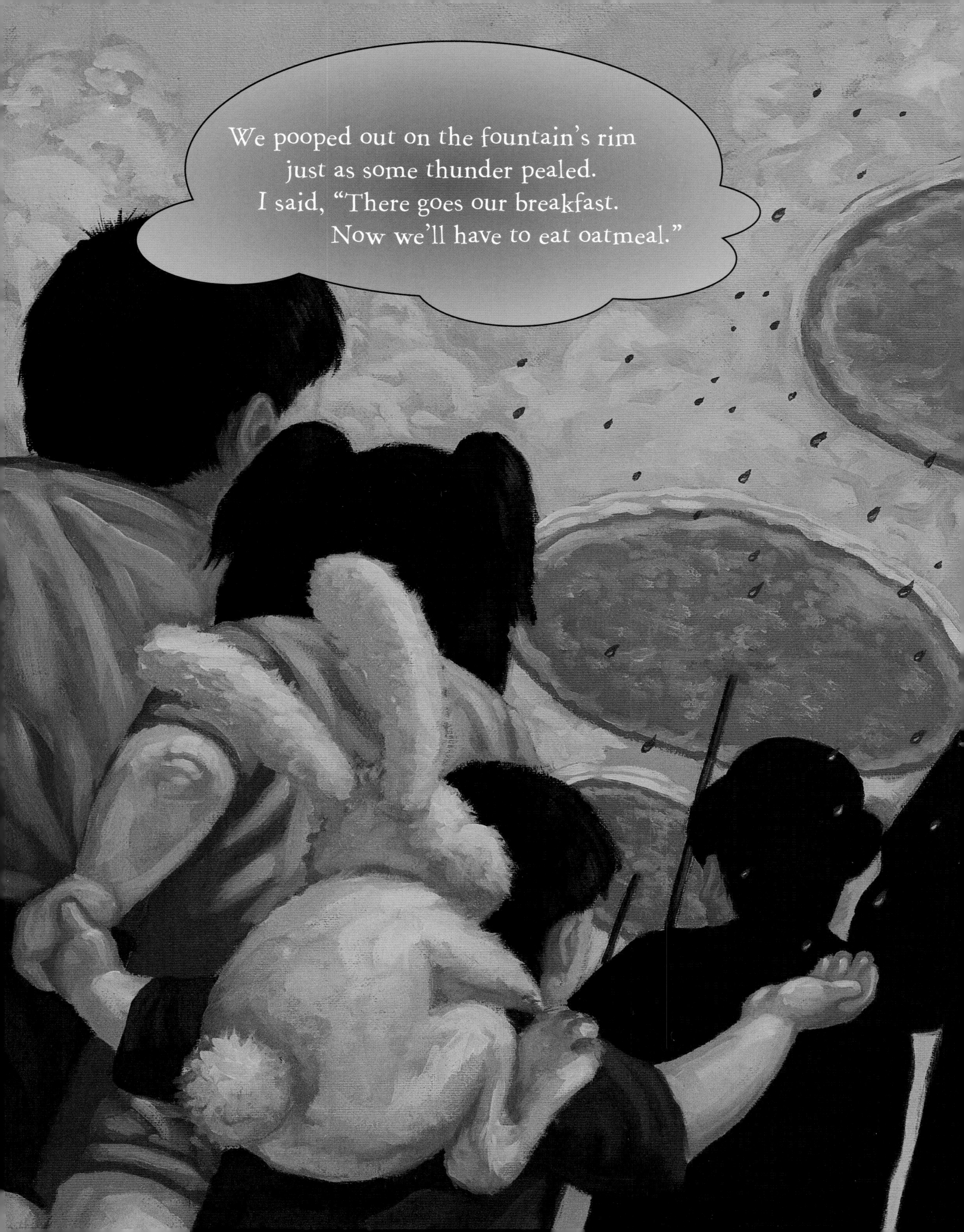
We pooped out on the fountain's rim
just as some thunder pealed.
I said, "There goes our breakfast.
Now we'll have to eat oatmeal."

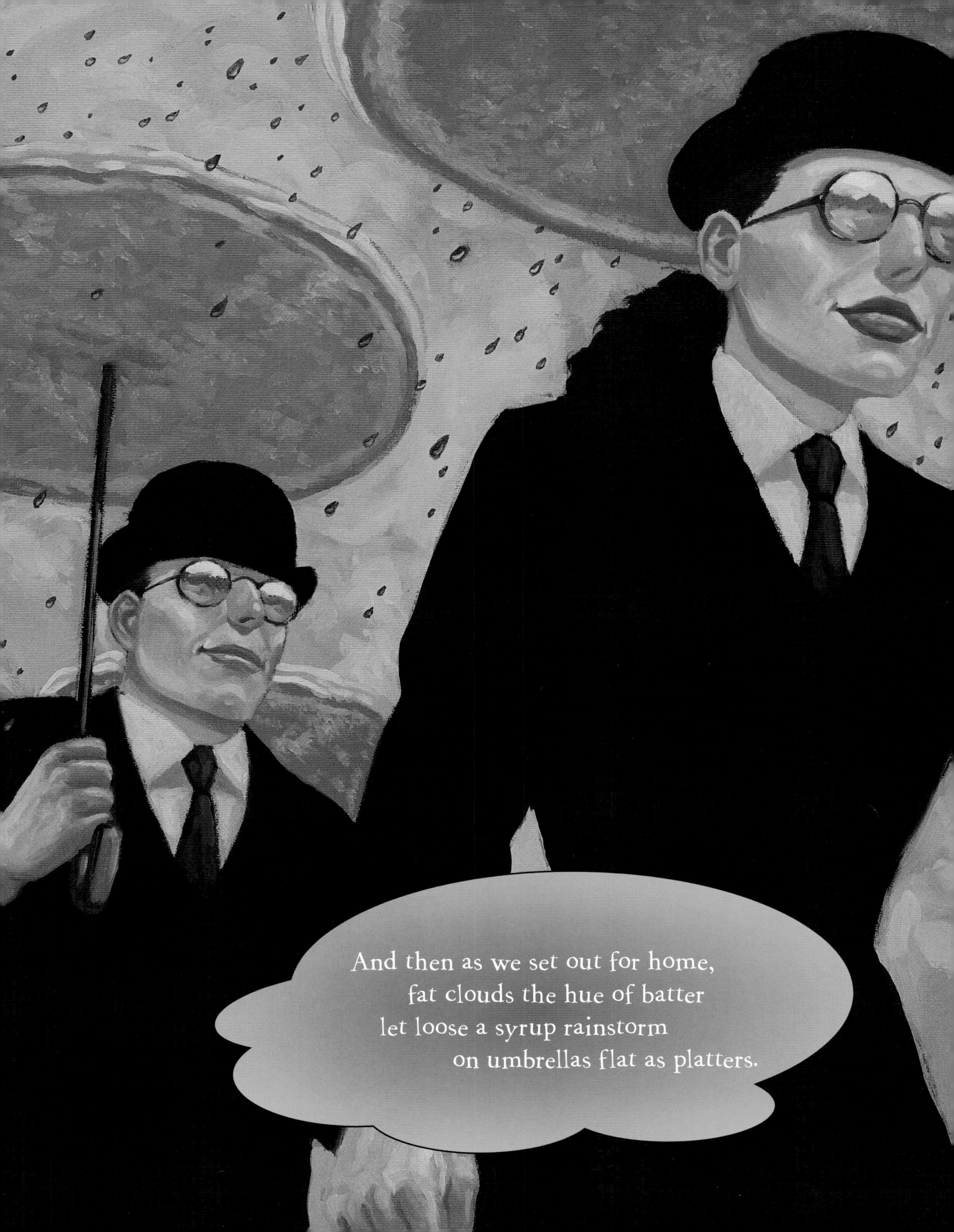

And then as we set out for home,
fat clouds the hue of batter
let loose a syrup rainstorm
on umbrellas flat as platters.

"Please help me find my specs," said Dad,
when we stumbled in the door.
But we found his old cookbook instead
—it had tumbled to the floor.

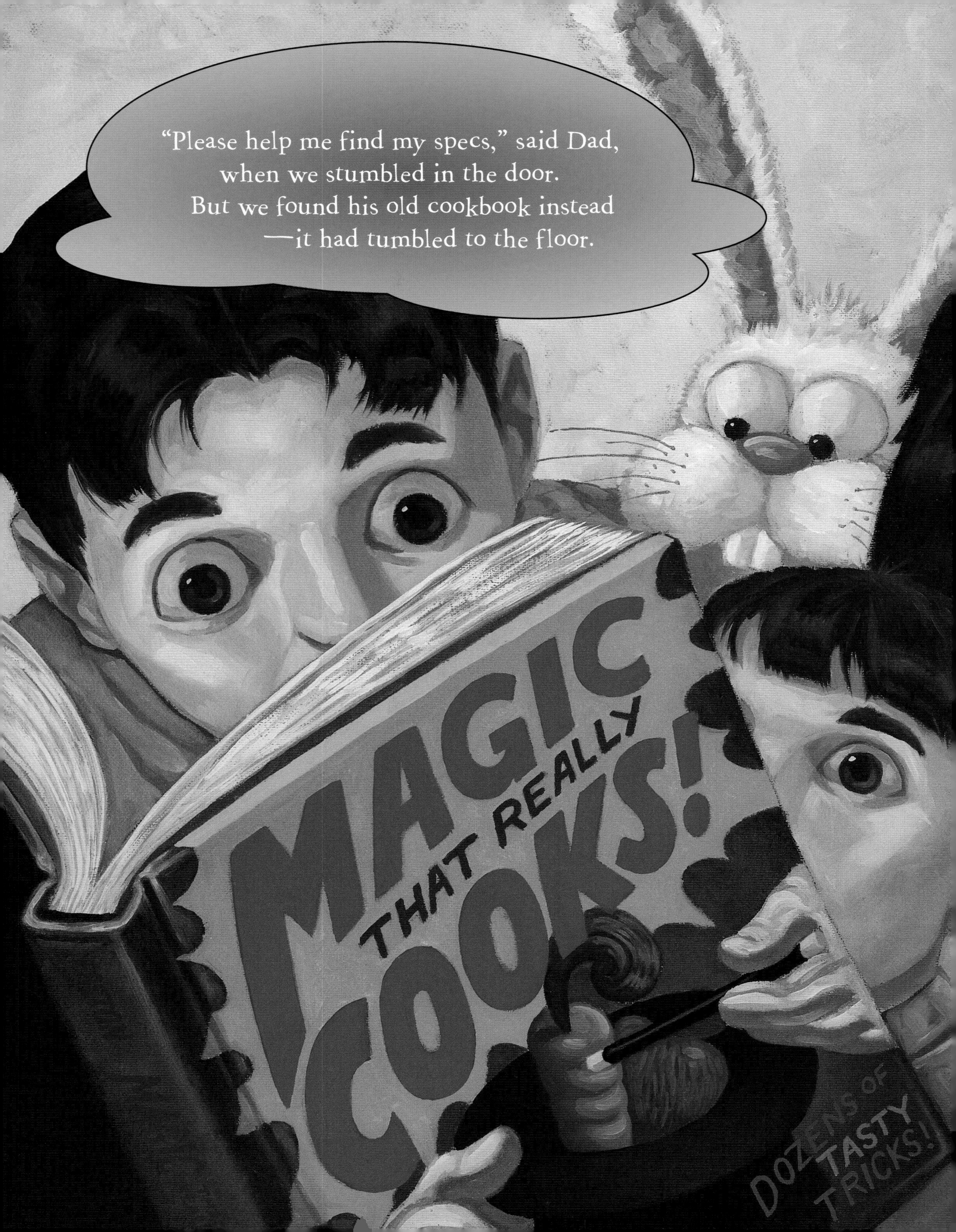
MAGIC
THAT REALLY
COOKS!
DOZENS OF
TASTY
TRICKS!

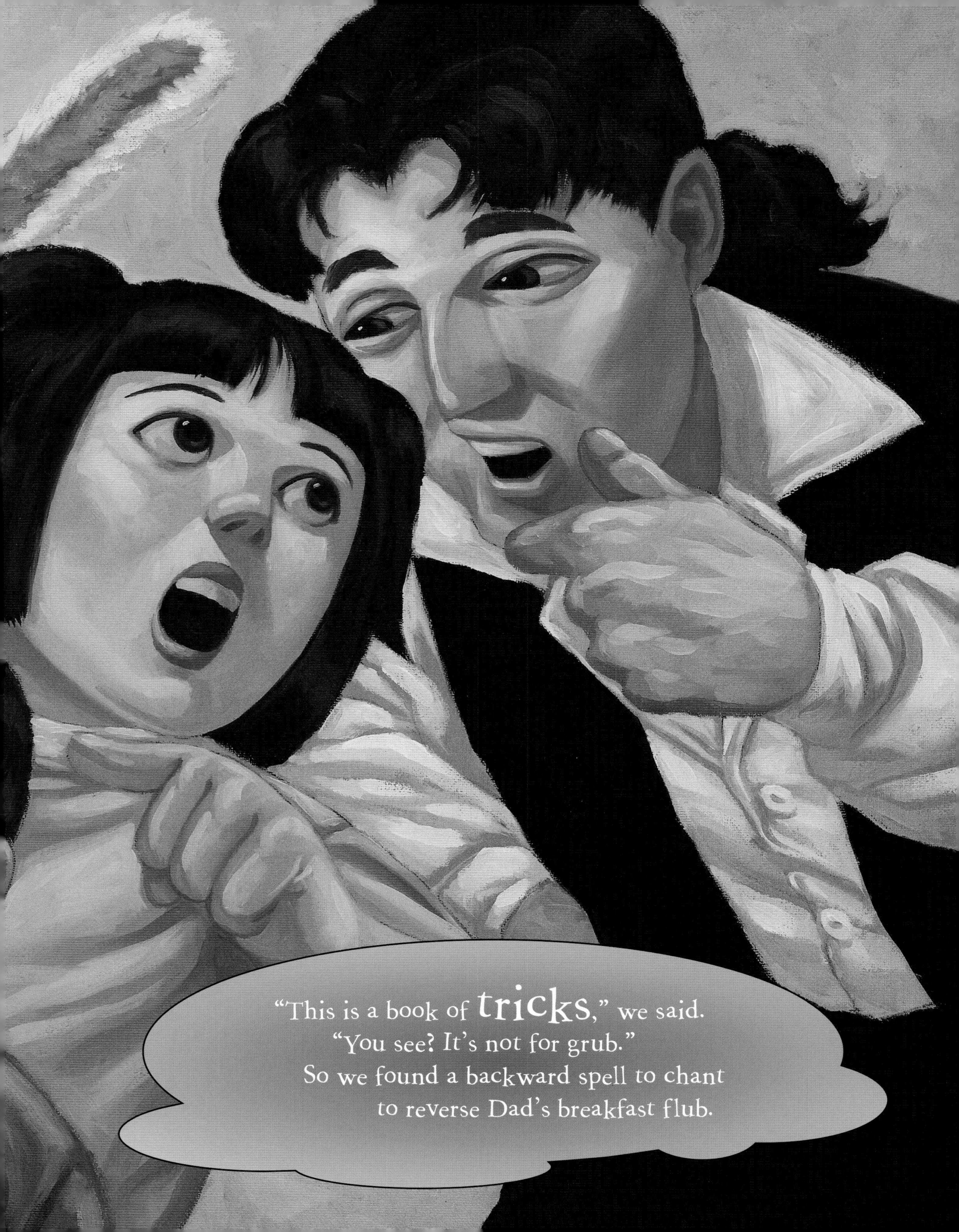

"This is a book of **tricks**," we said.
"You see? It's not for grub."
So we found a backward spell to chant
to reverse Dad's breakfast flub.

We all hollered

"OODOOH ƎKACTOH!"

Then we heard a MIGHTY ROAR,
an avalanche of cakes rolled down
and blasted through the door.

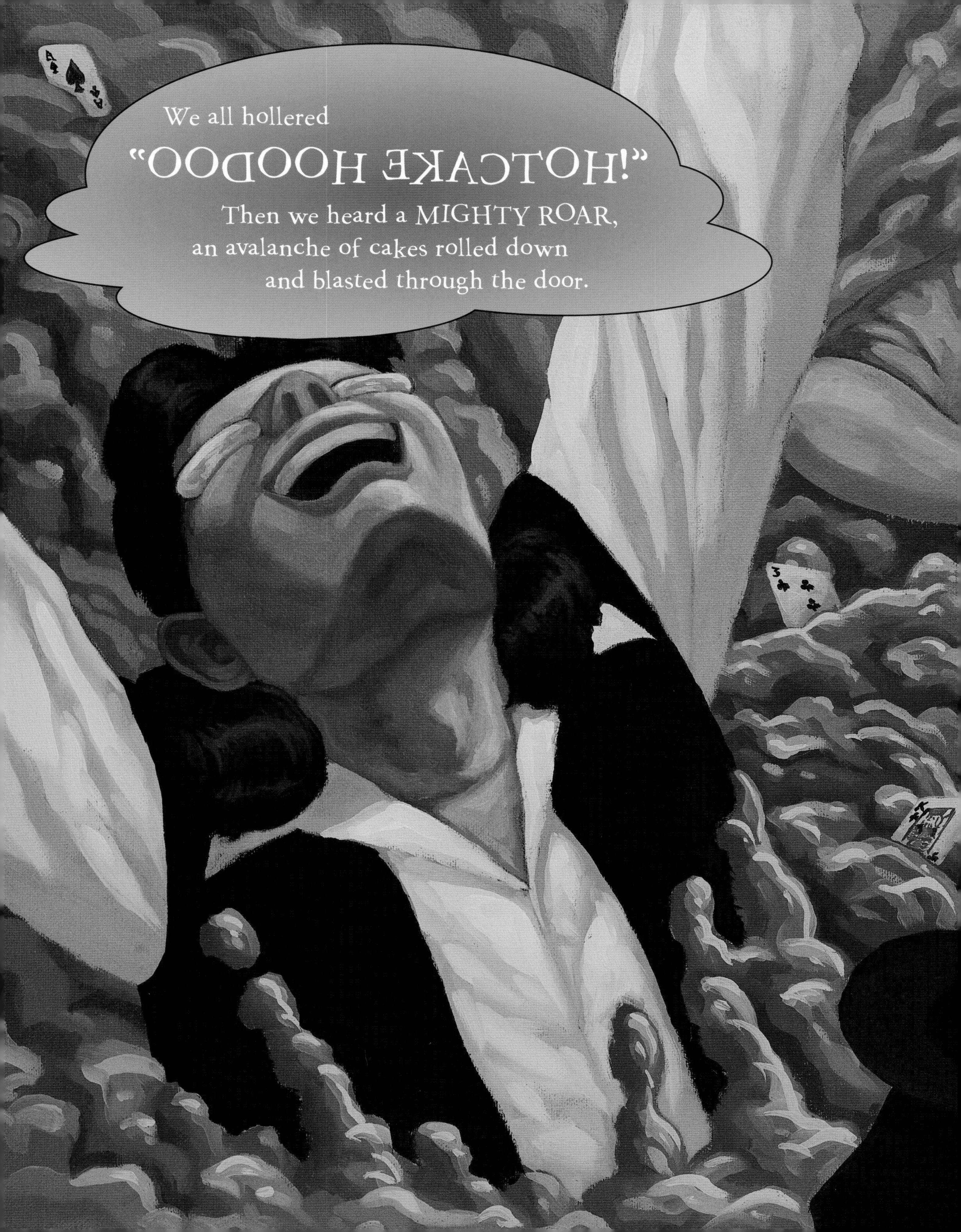

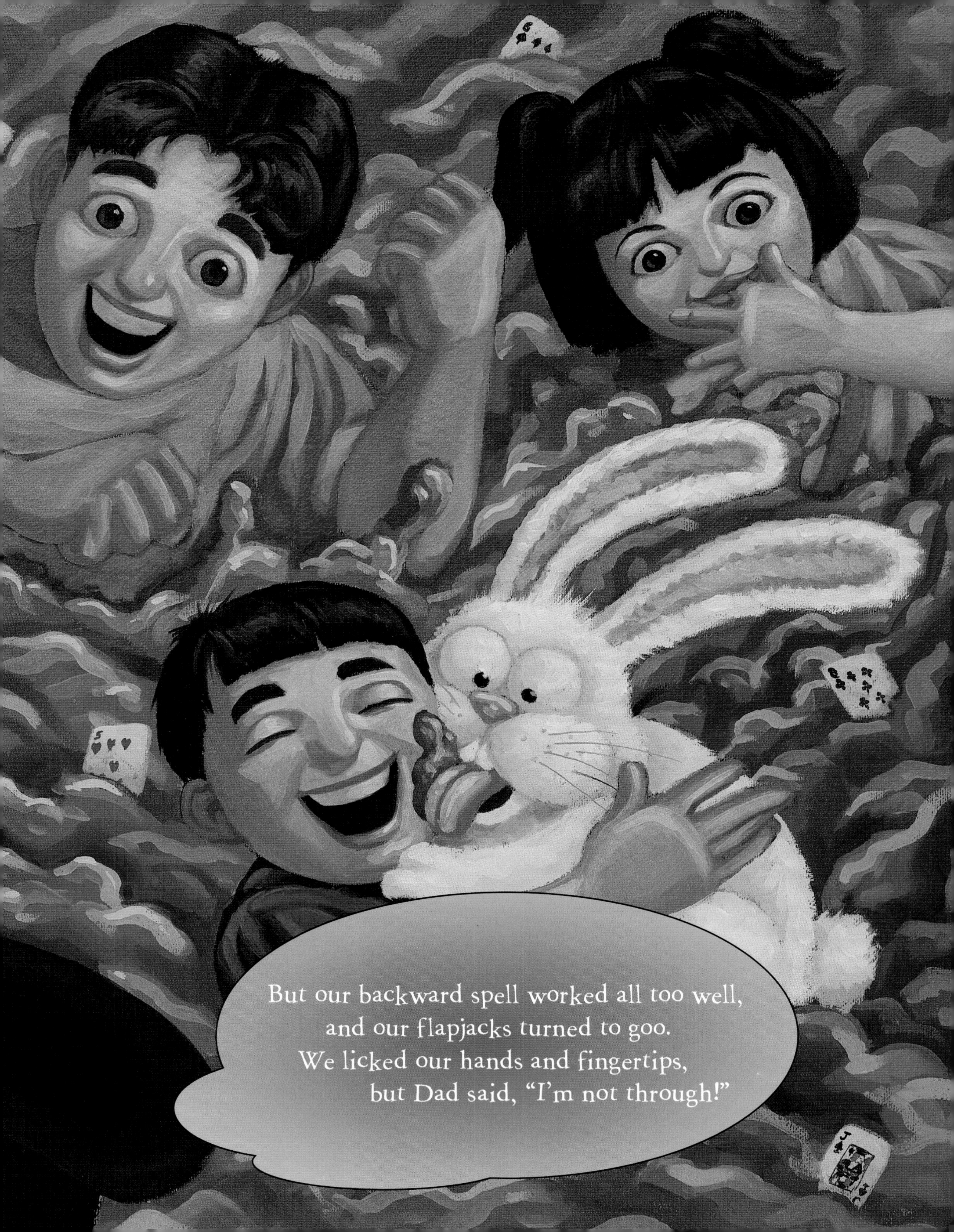

But our backward spell worked all too well,
and our flapjacks turned to goo.
We licked our hands and fingertips,
but Dad said, "I'm not through!"

“I’ll fry you up another stack.”
But we said, “No! Just watch!”
Then we toasted frozen waffles
right from the soggy box.

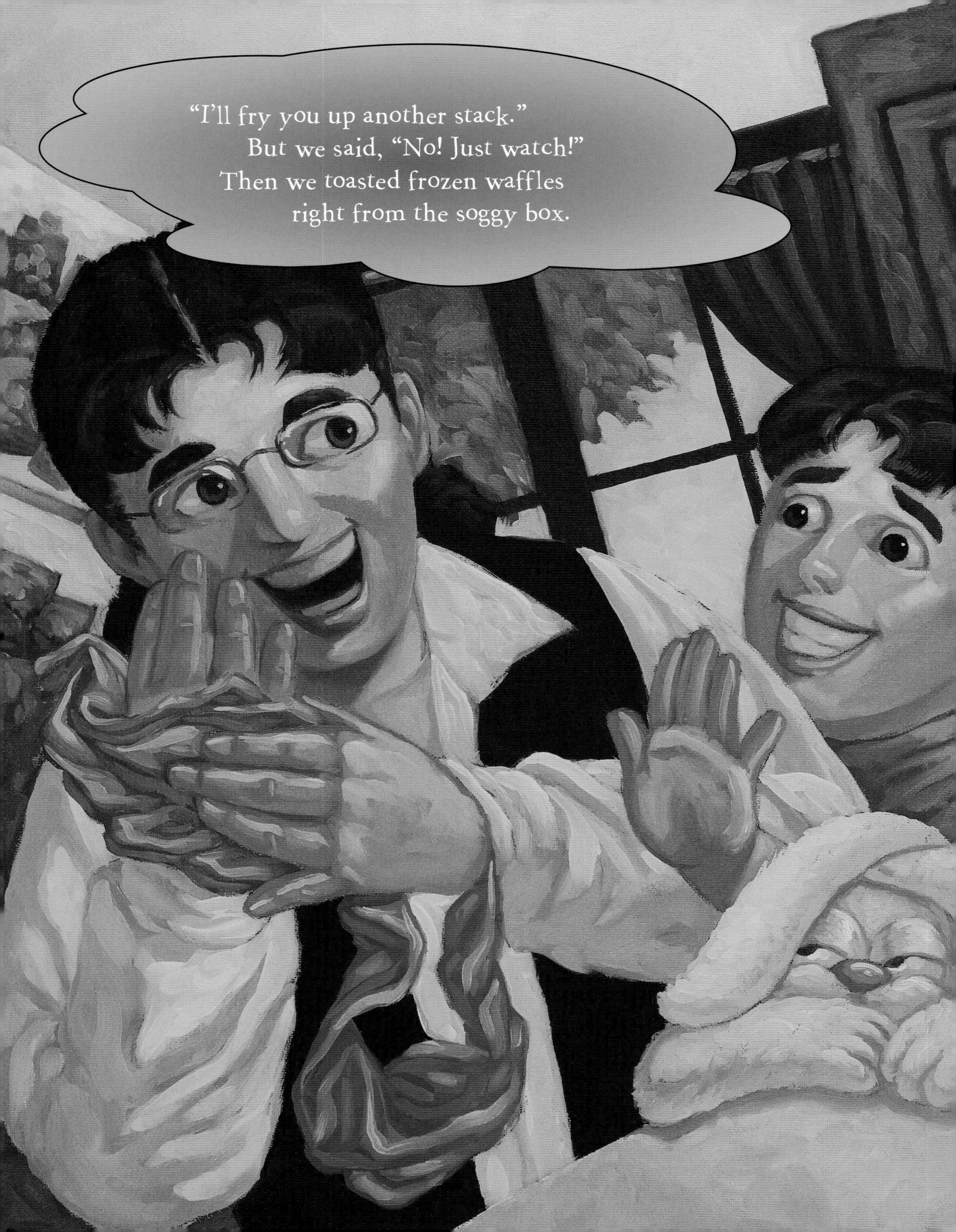

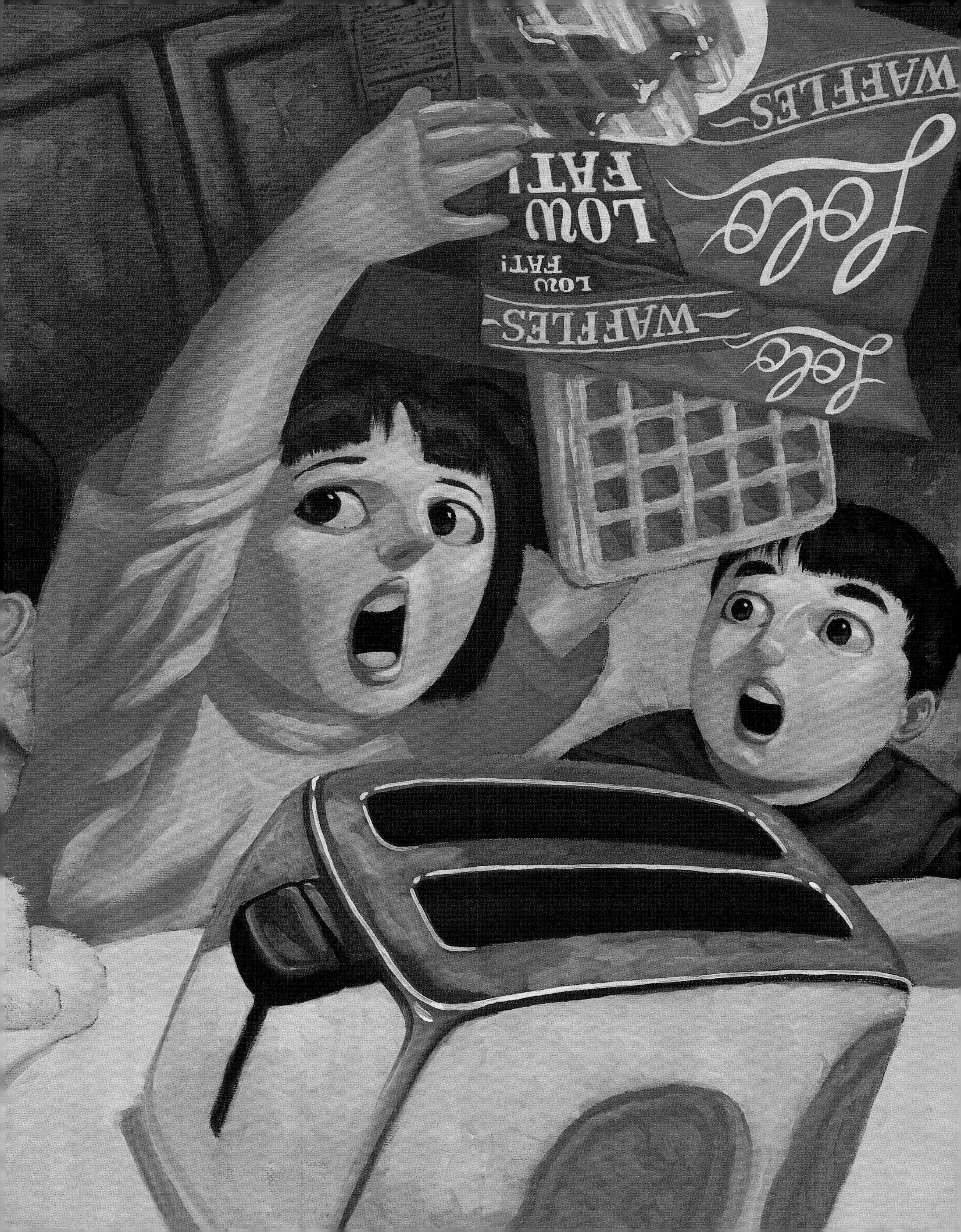
Lolo
WAFFLES
LOW FAT!
Lolo
WAFFLES
LOW FAT!

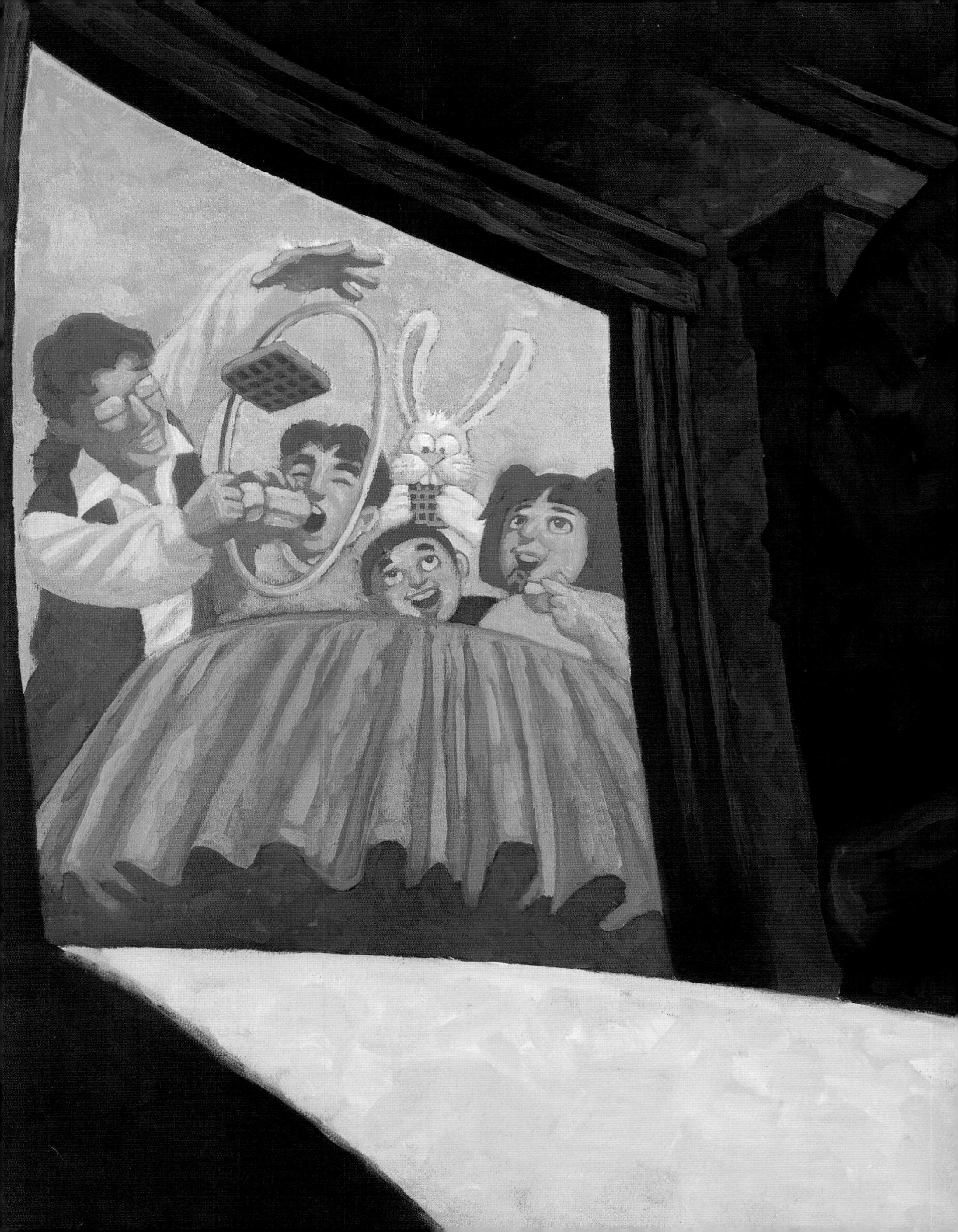

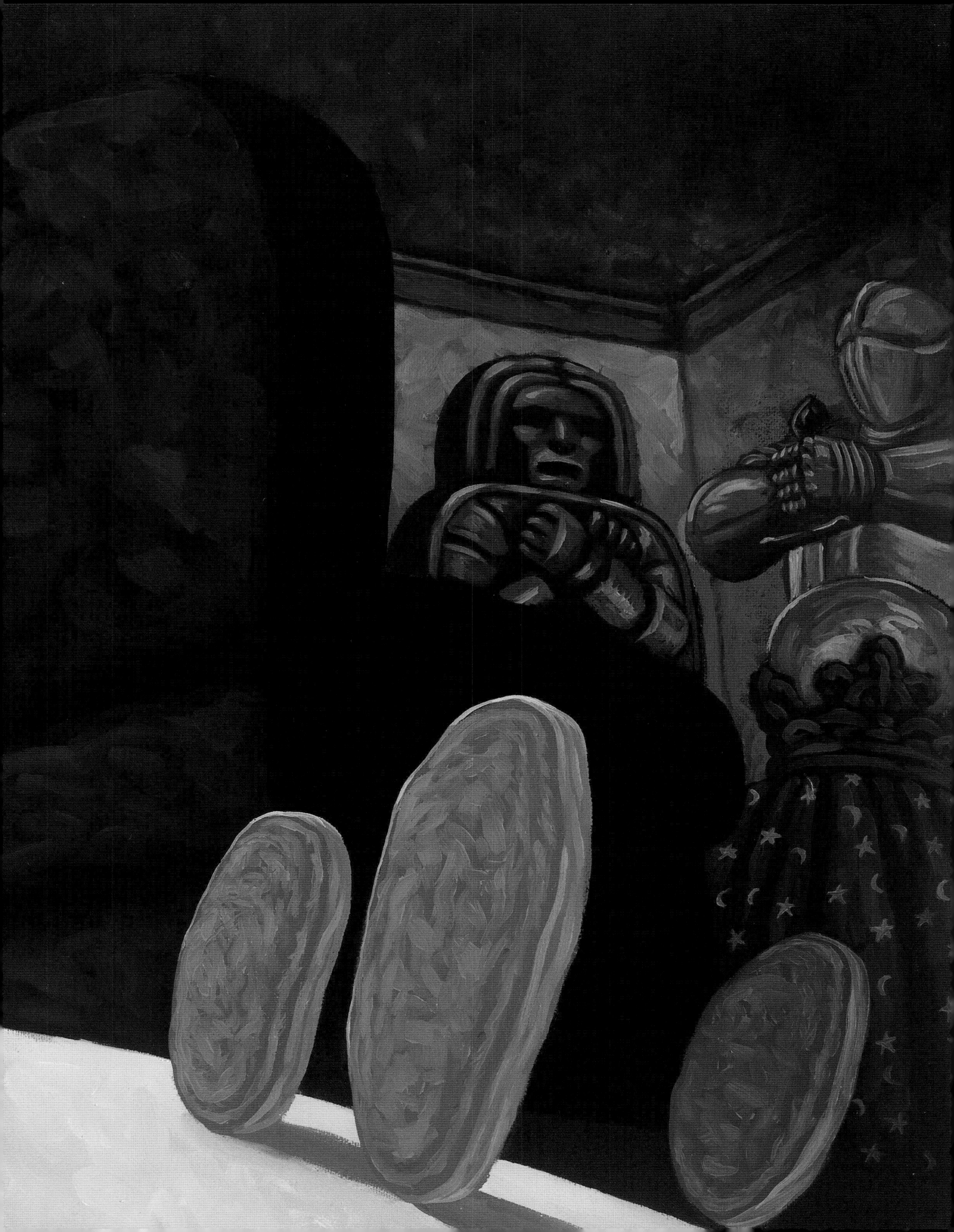

To Reed and Gwen who love my blueberry pancakes. —P. M.
For my niece, Aleix Yukiko, and my nephew, Michael Michio. —S. G.

Author's Note: For added fun, you may sing the verses in this book to the tune of "O, Susanna." Here's the chorus: "Pancakes! Pancakes! / Oh don't you fly from me. / For I haven't had my breakfast and my stomach is emp-ty."

Text copyright © 2002 by Paul Many
Illustrations copyright © 2002 by Scott Goto

First published in the United States of America in 2002 by Walker Publishing Company, Inc.

Published simultaneously in Canada by Fitzhenry and Whiteside, Markham, Ontario L3R 4T8

Library of Congress Cataloging-in-Publication Data

Many, Paul.
   The great pancake escape / Paul Many; illustrations by Scott Goto.
      p.   cm.
   Summary: When a magician accidentally uses the wrong book to make pancakes,
his children are led on a merry chase through town trying to catch their wiggly, sneaky breakfast.
   ISBN 0-8027-8795-9 — ISBN 0-8027-8796-7 (reinforced)
   [1. Pancakes, waffles, etc.—Fiction. 2. Cookery—Fiction. 3. Magic—Fiction.
4. Magicians—Fiction. 5. Stories in rhyme.] I. Goto, Scott, ill. II. Title.

PZ8.3.M3573 Gr2002
[E]—dc2l

                                                          2001026587

Book design by Sophie Ye Chin

Printed in Hong Kong
10 9 8 7 6 5 4 3 2 1

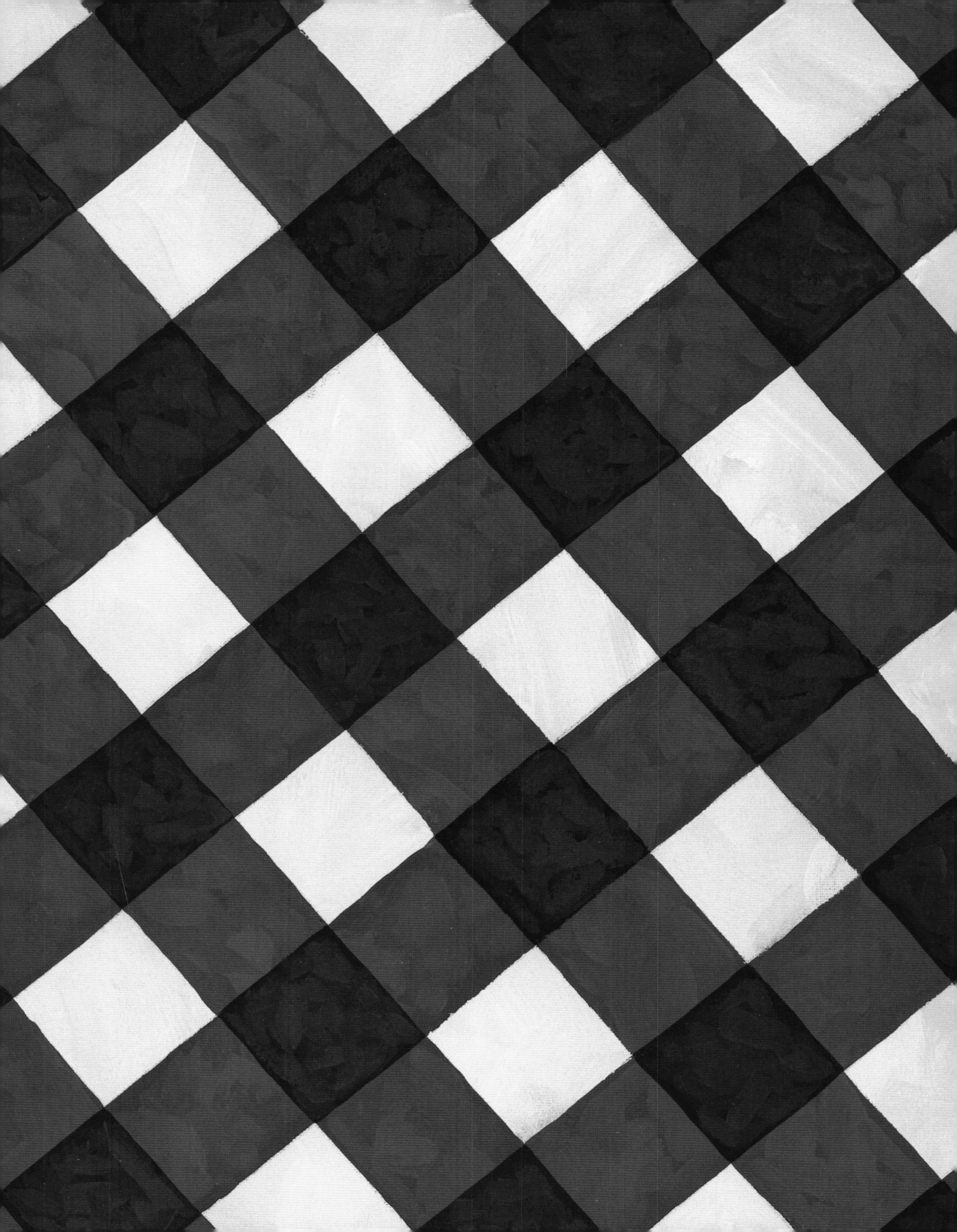